PROTECTED

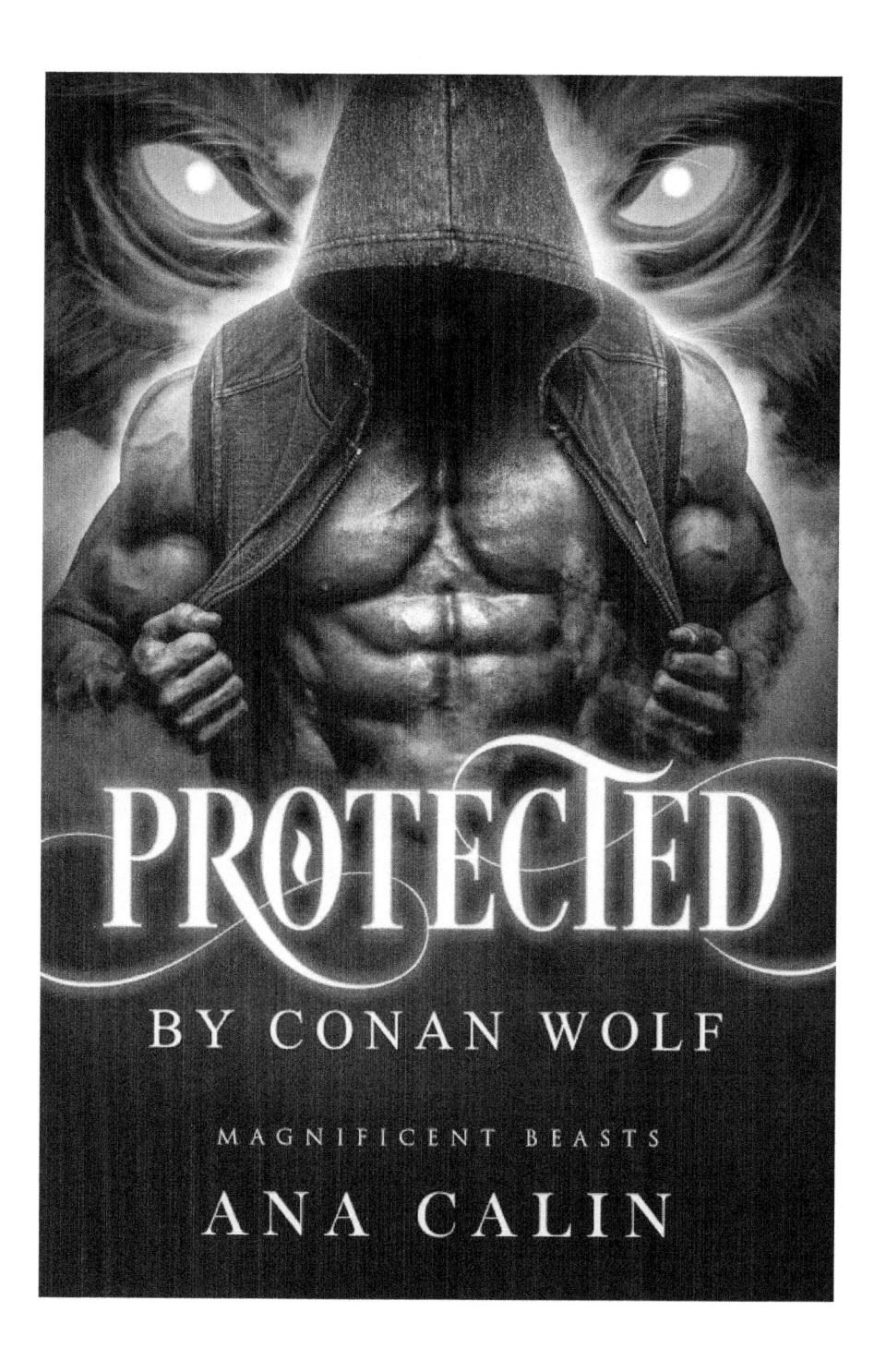

BY CONAN WOLF

MAGNIFICENT BEASTS

ANA CALIN

ALL RIGHTS RESERVED
No part of this book may be reproduced or transmitted in
any form or by any means, electronic or mechanical,
including photocopying, recording, or by any information storage
and retrieval system, without permission in writing
from the author except in the case of brief quotations
embodied in reviews.
Publisher's Note:
This is a work of fiction,
the work of the author's imagination.
Any resemblance to real persons or events is
coincidental.

———————

Copyright July 2019 – Ana Calin

Table of Contents

Title Page 1
Copyright Page 2
CHAPTER I 4
CHAPTER II 14
CHAPTER III 26
CHAPTER IV 39
CHAPTER V 56
CHAPTER VI 72
CHAPTER VII 95

CHAPTER I

Janine

I'VE SEEN THE HUGE Conan Wolf around Darkwood Falls quite a few times since the werewolves settled in, but I only saw him up close earlier today. He pulled up in the driveway of my hotel deep in the woods, stepped out of his SUV, came to my office and stated that, starting today, he would be my bodyguard.

"The serpent shifters are out to impregnate the Fated Females of Darkwood Falls," he said in a deep gritty voice. "We sealed the town, but you live outside its borders, and you travel a lot. You either give that up and move back into town, or you'll have me around at all times. Just so that we're understood, I will install cameras in all your private chambers, including your bathroom, because serpents can infiltrate through pipes and holes. You'll have *no* privacy at all. So what will it be?"

I squared my shoulders, mustering all of my businesswoman confidence.

"I won't be able to run a chain of hotels and keep an active public image by sealing myself off from the world."

"Then I'll settle in," he decreed. "I'll take a room on the same floor as yours."

He turned around and stalked off, without asking my opinion, hell, without even asking whether a room on my floor was even available. He ignored the elevators where a group of guests waited, and started up the stairs, a backpack slung over his shoulder. Everybody stared, staff and guests, but they all kept clear of him.

And who could blame them? Conan Wolf is a beast with muscles bulging through the sleeves of his black V-neck, the cleft between his pectorals so starkly defined he seems made of boulders. A scar cuts through his eyebrow and runs down to his hard mouth, and it wouldn't surprise me if he could splinter rocks with his jaw. My bff Arianna saw him shift once, and she said he turns into a brown wolf with eyes like fire. She saw him break through the outer brick wall of her bedroom, and now that I've seen him up close, I wonder how come her house is still standing.

I spent all day thinking about how Conan Wolf is similar to and yet different from his brothers. While the others are drop-dead gorgeous, it's his size and the brutality of his face that strike instead of his beauty. I'm looking for an online profile of him as we speak, wanting to see more of his face and analyze it, because I was too proud to stare at him face to face, when there's a powerful knock on my door.

I desperately click the x in the tab. Too late, *Conan Wolf* is still in the search bar when he enters. Luckily he can only see the metallic grey lid of my laptop from where he stands, and I manage to click it away before he strides to my desk. The man is so big he seems to fill the room. He holds out what looks like a fancy letter, some kind of invitation like the one I got a few years ago from TEDx, inviting me to speak at one of their events.

"You opened it." I can't keep the edge from my voice as I take the envelope from his hand. "Bodyguard or not, you don't get to open my mail or go through my—"

"Get used to it, Miss Kovesi," he cuts me off. "I will be violating your privacy on a regular basis in order to protect you. And your personal mail is the first thing I'll check daily."

Aaaand, there it is—the electrifying sensation up my back. It's a big secret, but it turns me on when men become domineering. I cross my legs under the desk and squirm against my own thighs, my eyes cast down on the open envelope to avoid Conan seeing my blush. I open the invitation, my eyes widening as I read the lines carved into the classy cardstock paper.

"Lord Lorenzo Piovra," Conan begins explaining as I read the letter, "is one of the most powerful alphas in Europe. He runs the werewolf pack in Venice, and his tentacles spread out to the whole of Italy—the center of werewolf power in Europe. Actually, Piovra isn't his real name, it's a name that developed over the centuries. It means octopus, and it describes what his pack truly is. An octopus that wants to grab the whole of Europe in its tentacles."

"Why does he want to see me of all people?" I lower the invitation.

Conan's russet eyes narrow. "I don't know yet, but I will find out. One thing is clear, though—if Lorenzo Piovra wants to meet you, it's because you're special."

"Special?" I arch an eyebrow. "How am I more special than the rest of Darkwood Falls?"

"We don't know that yet. All we have are suspicions. But one thing is clear, this is happening because of the serpents," Conan grunts under his breath, his eyes flashing blood red in the evening light as he re-reads Lord Piovra's invitation. "They made too much noise, and now all the werewolf clans found out about Darkwood Falls. This place was supposed to remain secret, a safe haven."

"But more werewolf clans knowing also means more help against the serpents."

"Yes, but it mostly means more power-mongering alphas fighting over control."

I narrow my eyes. "When your brother Nero came to this town as interim mayor, he said he wasn't interested in controlling the town, but in protecting it."

"I admit I think differently." Conan squares his shoulders, looking even bigger. "Nero is our alpha, and a very capable one, but there are things he doesn't understand or refuses to accept. He's a strategist, a superbrain, I'm a soldier. I've seen enough to know that powerful people always hunger for more power, and they'll stop at nothing to get it. Nero likes to see the good in all werewolves, and he sometimes underestimates our beastly drives. He thinks all werewolves are as well developed spiritually as him, but that's simply not the case."

He looks out the window, as if assessing a distant danger. "And now that of all the alphas Lorenzo Piovra has found out about Darkwood Falls, things are going to get especially ugly. This town holds a much-desired resource in the werewolf world—Fated Females. There's a shortage all over the globe, so Piovra must have already decided he'll take over. He just needs a good reason to attack."

I get up from my chair, heading over to Conan. I place one foot in front of the other carefully, imagining myself prancing on a catwalk. Damn, I don't think I ever wanted to impress a man more than I want to impress Conan Wolf now. The closer I come to him, the faster my pulse. I lean with my shoulder against the window on the side opposite to him.

"Would the lives of the town's people be any worse under Lorenzo Piovra than under Nero? Why should we care who gets to control this town if the werewolves will protect us anyway?" I won't get into a feminist rage about women being seen as commodities, not right now.

Conan looks into my face. The evening light falls on those hard features in a way that I find very much to my liking. I shift my weight from one foot to the other and cross my arms, hoping to hide the way he makes me feel. I take the chance to explore his brutish face. He may not be every girl's dream husband, but I'm sure he's every girl's secret wet dream.

"Not all werewolf alphas are like Nero, Miss Kovesi. Kind and human-loving, I mean. They would protect the Fated Females, yes, and maybe all of the town's people in the hope that they'll produce more of those females, but it would be a regime of terror."

I motion with my chin to Lorenzo's invitation between his hands.

"Okay, so Lorenzo Piovra found out about Darkwood Falls and Fated Females. Why do you suppose he wrote to me of all people? I don't even know for sure if I'm a Fated Female."

"Like I said, all I have right now is theories. But it could be because of your position in Darkwood Falls."

"My position?" I snort. "Don't be fooled by my successful business. I'm not an aristocrat like Arianna and Princess. My family worked their way to power and money. Business runs in my blood, but I'm no aristocrat. I'm not even a decision maker in this town, none of my family are members of the Council, so what could someone like Lorenzo Piovra have to gain from me?"

Conan folds his big arms across his chest. The man is a freaking colossus, making me feel like an anorexic compared to him.

"We need to find that out. Maybe if you take some time to think about it you'll find a lead. You've already proven your detective skills."

I lift an eyebrow. "Good to see you value other qualities in a woman, other than her being a Fated Female."

"I wasn't talking about how I or any members of my pack view you. But how other werewolves will, especially ones as greedy for power as Lorenzo Piovra."

I stare at him, thinking. "Let's get Nero here."

※

Conan

"IT COULD BE MANY THINGS," Nero says, pacing Janine's office. The blonde businesswoman with the shiny bob is sitting at her desk, watching him, circling her stilettoed foot in the air. Her cobalt blue irises ooze so much intelligence that I can't look away.

"Could be something in your past that is of special interest to him, so let's talk about it," Nero argues.

A good thing he's only talking to her, and not me, because I'm no longer listening. Not actively anyways. I'm looking at Janine, trying to understand what it is that I'm sensing about her.

If I were a normal man, a human, the first thing I'd notice would be her powerful-woman kind of attractiveness. I wonder if she even knows how sexy she is. I think not. She dresses much too somber. I mean look at her now in her pencil skirt, with her shiny blonde bob and the perfectly arched eyebrows. She has a delicate heart-shaped face, but cobalt blue eyes that demand respect, and rather thin lips—not the kind of woman you imagine lustfully sucking you off. Unless you're me. My cock twitches, and I shake the thought away.

I'm sure Janine Kovesi scares men, especially because she's so interesting. No doubt she has many admirers from afar who prefer to jerk off to her IG profile than actually making a move on her. But there's more to this woman than her powerful kind of attractiveness. Something I sniffed when I assessed her body chemistry, something that told me she had something others didn't. Like a superpower she might not even know about.

"Well, there's only one way to find out why Lorenzo Piovra invited me to Venice," Janine says, standing up from her desk. "Asking him personally. I'm accepting his invitation."

"No way," I react. "It could be a trap. And more than just dangerous for you, Miss Kovesi, it could be deadly."

Janine's face hardens. Clearly, the woman isn't used to restrictions, which puts thoughts in my head of me submitting her to mine. My cock reacts, and I can barely keep it tame.

"Mr. Wolf," she stresses. "The first thing you told me when you walked into my office earlier today was that I would be able to keep travelling if I accepted you as my bodyguard. So come along as my protector, it's that simple."

"No, it's not," Nero counters. "Conan is the most experienced fighter of our pack, but he can't take the entire Piovra clan down by himself if things get nasty."

"Why would things get nasty?" Princess, Nero's soon-to-be wife, intervenes as she enters Janine's office with a tray of coffee cups. "The Piovras wouldn't want to start a war with the Wolf pack, would they? Because that's what would happen if they attacked Conan."

"A reason to start a war might be exactly what they're after," Nero argues. "And what better way than to make us attack first?"

"But if I refuse the invitation, they could use that as a pretext as well," Janine puts in, and she's right. "Maybe I'm not special at all, maybe they just chose me randomly, knowing you wouldn't expose any human from Darkwood Falls to danger, especially not a Fated Female, if I am one."

"Still, it wouldn't be reason enough," Nero says, but I've made my decision.

"I'll go with you, Miss Kovesi. So debate closed."

"What the hell, Conan?" Nero reacts, ready to decree against it, but luckily that's not how it works between us.

"If the Piovras are looking for trouble, they're going to find it one way or the other," I remind Nero. "I'll do my best to avoid conflict while I'm there and, if they cross the line, I'll sneak Miss Kovesi and myself out, and ignore my impulses to break their bones. Besides, this might be the only way for us to find out in what way Miss Kovesi is special." *Because she is, and you sniffed it out just like I did*, but Nero understands that without me saying it out loud.

"There's one other question that won't let me be," Janine says, eyes like slits as she sifts through her thoughts. "Why did I get this letter on the very day that Conan Wolf becomes my bodyguard?"

Nero normally he has at least a theory or two in place in a matter of minutes, but I see this puzzles him, too.

"Quite a few mysteries," Princess whispers, sipping her coffee.

"And I have a hunch there is only one answer to them all," Janine puts in. "Mr. Wolf." She points her chin at me, so we all know which one of us she means. "Have you ever met this Lorenzo before? Do you have old grudges?"

"Why do you ask?" Princess says. Janine's eyes narrow on me, intelligence shining out of them.

"The inflections in his voice when he says the name Piovra. Like he's spitting it. I know a grudge when I hear one."

Memories crawl up from the back of my mind. A sour taste fills my mouth, and my jaw clenches.

Janine

CONAN WOLF ISN'T A man of many words. But he did give us the short version of his and Lorenzo's history, and I'm still hanging out here with an open mouth thinking about it.

Conan Wolf and Lorenzo Piovra fought side by side in a serpent ambush that the Brigade of the Wolves—something like their kind's defense department—organized in the Alps two centuries ago. They managed to infiltrate the Reaper's very lair and, while the great Reaper escaped, they found his secret weapon hidden in the cave he'd left in haste, under what was left of an altar of the Serpent God.

It was a weapon that could "only be earned or given," that's how Conan put it. Conan and Lorenzo ended up fighting each other over it, and Conan won, thus 'earning' the weapon, but Lorenzo never came to terms with that. Over the past two centuries, Lorenzo kept trying to challenge Conan, picking fights so that he could reclaim the weapon. But neither of them ever told anyone what exactly that infamous weapon was. Conan never even told his brothers, who didn't pester with questions, because that is the level of depth, wisdom and understanding in their family.

It's late now, and I'm still turning the story around in my head. Princess stayed with me, while Nero and Conan went to prepare a strategy with their brothers at Drago's house. They left a whole squad of werewolves undercover to protect the hotel, which makes me feel like a little princess in an ivory tower. Can't say I mind, but—

"They should have taken us along," I tell Princess as I stare out the window. "I proved a good asset to them in matters of research and strategy last time, didn't I?"

"Yes, love, but the five brothers have been a compact cell for many centuries. They're used to discussing matters amongst themselves at first and, while Nero and Drago would take their bonded mates with them everywhere, the other three haven't imprinted yet, and they're different that way."

I wish I could bring a counter-argument, but I know she's right.

"I hope he comes back soon," I say, staring out into the night. "Conan, I mean. The werewolves hide well, but still. I don't want them around the hotel too much, the guests might notice something is wrong."

"The guests have always known something isn't quite right about Darkwood Falls, Janine, it's what draws them here," Princess says as she joins me by the window. "I think it's what really brings the tourists to this town. I mean, the landscape with the mountains, woods and falls are like from a fairy tale, but then again, there are other places like this in the States. People come here for the sense of mystery, of timelessness, of...."

"Power." I whisper while she ponders. She snaps her fingers.

"Yes, that's it."

"Especially since the werewolves," I say, eyes on the mountain contours. "Ever since Drago first set foot in this hotel and laid eyes on Arianna I felt like, I don't know, like immortality entered the town, but also brought death closer than ever."

"Hold your horses. There is no talk of immortality for Fated Females."

"Fated Females have to be immortal, especially those that werewolves have imprinted on." I walk away from the window and lean against the bedpost. "Can you imagine Drago without Arianna? He stares at her like an adoring puppy. You and Nero are another example. You haven't been together long, but—"

"Only one day, officially." A blissful smile lights up her face.

"Only one day, but he already loves you deeply. He's been waiting for his own 'The One' for centuries, how do you think he'd feel if he lost you in fifty years?"

"I guess he's living too strongly in the Now to think about that, and I don't fear death, Janine."

"Probably because you feel deep down there will be no death for you, not now that a werewolf has imprinted on you." Then it hits me. "Such a sad idea, if you think about it."

"Sad?" Princess' eyebrows rise. "Why would immortality be *sad*?"

"It's sad that a woman's salvation from death should come only through the love of a man. It's unfair, too."

"First of all, we don't know for a fact that's how things are, it's just speculation. Secondly, what is there to live forever for if not for love?" She grabs my shoulders, fixing me with those caramel eyes that go beautifully with her red locks. "Janine, if you felt about a man the way I feel about Nero, you'd see the world in a whole new light. Everything makes sense, the sand on the beaches, the clouds in the sky, the cool feel of rain on your face. It's like every experience in your life has led up to this moment, to this man, to this love you feel." She shakes her head, her hands dropping off me. "I wish I could explain it better."

The feelings I read in her face, the bliss, the joy, the selflessness, they're fascinating.

"I'm happy for you, and envious at the same time," I whisper. "I wish I could feel all that. At least for a moment."

"I wish it for you as well. It's quite the experience."

I swallow hard. I've been alone for so long.

"Now," she says with a girlish grin, as if she's been dying to ask me all along. "Nero has sent Conan to be your bodyguard, how sexy is that? Doesn't he, you know, make you feel something out of the ordinary?"

I hate admitting it, but I need to tell someone.

"I like him. He is—" I hesitate. "Quite a specimen."

"Quite a specimen? The guy is downright wow."

"And fear-inducing."

"Don't tell me you don't find that sexy."

"Listen, before you get all excited that three best friends will end up mated with three hot werewolves," I say with grit in my voice, "let me tell you I'm not as crazy about Conan as you were about Nero, or Arianna about Drago. He's a magnificent beast, and I'd fuck the daylights out of him, but that's far from love at first sight or anything of the kind."

Princess winks and taps her nose with her index finger. "Believe me, after you've fucked him, you'll want more and more. That's how it began for Arianna and me, too. Remember, Arianna found Drago insanely attractive in the beginning, but she didn't fall in love at first sight. She didn't even want to sleep with him because she was afraid she'd be too needy afterwards, but it was him who fell for her like a madman. I was crazily attracted to Nero, too, but love didn't hit me like lightning. It was off-the-charts sexual attraction at first."

"It's off-the-charts sexual attraction for me, too. If I were to act purely on my desires, I'd sweep everything off my desk and open my legs for him right there. But..." I bite my lip, my cheeks heating up. "I'm afraid he'd reject me."

Princess frowns, motioning for me to sit with her on the bed. "Why would he do that?"

"Because he's not attracted to me. He looked at me so coldly I might as well have been a piece of furniture. Plus, he said he wasn't interested in imprinting."

"When did he say that?"

"While we were waiting for you and Nero to arrive. I asked him if I was a Fated Female. He sniffed at me a few times, and said I was, but didn't show the slightest interest."

Princess's frown deepens. "Hmm, I wonder how come. Don't all werewolves naturally and instinctively want to imprint on a woman, find their mate?"

"I don't know, but Conan said he was a soldier, not a lover. He steers clear of emotional attachment in order to focus on war. He's detached and calculating. And I don't think I'll be the woman to change that."

CHAPTER II

Janine

I thought it would be days, but weeks pass as we prepare for the trip to Venice. I draft an official response letter for Lorenzo under Nero's supervision, which we'll send through normal mail, which buys us more time. But then the communication moves to e-mail, going much faster. We agree that Lorenzo and I will meet at his palazzo in Venice in three weeks' time—yes, a palace.

At first I'm relieved, saying to Nero when we gather at his house for dinner, "That's a good sign, isn't it? If he's not in a hurry to meet me, doesn't press for things to happen right away, then—"

"It's not a good sign at all, it's a bad one," Conan interrupts. My eyes shift to him. He's sitting between his brothers Drago and Achilles on the other side of the table, a beast with muscles like boulders compared to them. A brute among his beautiful brothers, with his hard features and the scar running down the side of his face.

"Did you hear what I just said, Miss Kovesi," he addresses me a few moments later, waking me from the daydream of his large rough muscles against my body. I shake my head.

"I'm sorry, I wasn't paying attention."

"Yes, you looked rather distracted."

I take my hand to my cheek, looking down as he speaks, trying to hide the blush.

"It means Lorenzo Piovra is taking more time to prepare," Conan says. "He probably didn't expect you to accept his invitation, or he didn't expect that Nero, the alpha protector of this town, would let you travel to see him. The more I think about it, the more I believe he was just looking for a pretext to pick a fight with us. But now that you agreed to go to Venice, with nothing but one bodyguard—his longtime rival no less—he needs to go over the details of his plan." His eyes fill with red fire.

"Agreed," Nero says from the head of the table. "Which means we have to be prepared, too. I still don't understand how his invitation reached Janine on the very day you became her bodyguard, Conan, but I'm sure it wasn't a coincidence."

"We'll find out the truth behind all that," I say, getting a grip. I'm Janine Kovesi, a strong and independent woman, I won't break under the weight of lust like a schoolgirl. "That's why I'm going to meet Lord Piovra. But we should probably think up an escape plan in case all he wants is to trap Conan—because that's my theory; that he only used me in order to get to him. I think he somehow knew the pack wouldn't let me travel to Venice without him."

"I don't agree," Conan intervenes. "Even if getting me to Venice was his plan from the start, because there I would be on his territory, the letter needed time to reach us from Italy, so he wrote it before I became your bodyguard."

"Like I said, too many open questions and only one way to answer them all, namely my accepting his invitation." My eyes stay on Conan, but I address the others. "I have an idea how to keep Conan out of danger until we gauge Lorenzo's motives and intentions."

Everybody at the table stares at me.

"I will speak at a conference on the Cote d'Azure two days before the meeting in Venice. I get tons of invitations to speak at conferences, Conan knows. I think the location of this one is perfect, close to Venice so Lord Piovra can't refuse meeting me there. I can confirm my attendance tonight. That way Lorenzo, Conan and I won't have our first meeting on Piovra territory."

"I like that idea," Nero said.

"So do I," Conan adds, and I sit to attention against my best wishes. He sits like a soldier between his brothers, staring me in the face, and the skin on my spine tingles. "You are a brilliant woman, Miss Kovesi, I have to tell you that."

"Thank you," I mutter and look away. I don't want him to think I'm overly moved by his display of appreciation.

All the while we put together the details of the plan I'm hyper aware of Conan's eyes watching me. Get a grip, Janine, this doesn't mean he wants to kiss you and make babies.

But back at the hotel I still can't help prancing like a rookie model whenever I feel him staring at me. I'm usually busy with work and guests, always in my stiff two-piece suits, all cold and business-like, but a few times I do put on a dress, secretly wanting to be feminine and enticing for him.

Conan watches me from dark corners, often while talking on his phone. I can't know whether he likes what he sees or not, I only know he's doing his job, and he's doing it well.

As time passes my desire for him grows, until my body is basically screaming for him. He's been my bodyguard for almost five weeks now, always watching me, breathing down my nape. Stalking me, but not the way I want him to.

By the time we're together on a plane to France my hormones are killing me. And when we reach the hotel in Nice and Conan asks for a double room for us both, making it clear he'll be sharing with me, sweat breaks out on my back.

The concierge's eyes dart from me to the big scarred guy and back again, his thoughts clear in his long face that reminds me of a stuck up butler—a business woman and a muscle bound beast that don't share a last name; he probably thinks I'm cheating on my official guy with this one, especially since Conan bribes him to keep his name off the record. I can feel the concierge's questioning stare on my back as we head for the elevator.

The moment Conan pushes the door open and we walk into a fabulous room on the tenth floor, the floor-to-ceiling windows open and the sea breeze blowing through the white drapes, my need for him overflows and becomes painful. I drop my handbag, turn on my heel and confront him.

"Why, Conan? Why not take the room next door, like back home in Darkwood Falls? Can't you imagine what the concierge thinks of me now? He knows I'll be speaking at the conference, he knows who I am."

"First of all, I did it because we're not on our own territory anymore. Here danger could creep from every crack in the wall."

I look around and slap my hands on my thighs. "This is a five star hotel, there are no cracks in the walls."

He ignores my mockery. "Secondly, I wouldn't worry about our good old concierge. He'll be having a good time by himself thinking of you and me under the sheets together."

"Say what?"

He looks me up and down to make a point. I'm wearing a tight tank top with the top of my black lace bra peeking the hem. But I also have a light beige jacket over my shoulders. My usually perfectly styled blonde bob is now messy from the way I slept on the plane, and all I've done to style it was run my fingers through it on our taxi ride here.

"You're looking sexy today," Conan says like he's simply announcing the weather. "And I think you are his type. The concierge's."

"Oh really? And what type is that?"

"Sassy. Plus that you're softer after a plane flight, your hair isn't perfect, your clothes don't make you look like you're as off limits as the Queen, and your eyes are too tired to be cutting through men. That scares guys usually, but today the dosage is just perfect."

"Wow," I whisper. "So you can see things in women after all, we're not just pieces of furniture to you."

"No, sometimes you're roommates. But don't worry, we're only gonna be sharing a room for two nights. You'll be on stage at the conference tomorrow, then in the evening you'll meet Lorenzo. By nightfall you'll be too tired to even notice my presence. Then we'll be out of here."

He heads over to shut the window, drawing the drapes back together. I watch his back as his arms work, beautiful muscles snaking under his white T-shirt that stretches across the width of his shoulders. I catch a glimpse of his strong jaw as he looks to the side. It's the side with the scar that I find so sexy it's almost sick.

"Okay, maybe I should just be straight-forward with you," I say.

"Yes, maybe you should." He moves back to the bags, and hunkers down to open his, his jeans stretching over his muscular legs. I lick my lips.

"Ever since you came into my life I haven't, you know, I haven't been able to...." I freeze when he looks up at me, those reddish irises piercing.

"Yes," he nudges when I don't continue.

"You know what I mean, don't make me say it."

He stands back up to full height, my head moving up as he does. It's been five weeks, and he still doesn't cease to amaze me. The short sleeves of his white T-shirt stretch tight around his bicep, his pectorals bulging. And the face, that brutish but handsome face. An image of me straddling his face hits me, and I squeeze my thighs together where I stand.

Conan catches it. Damn it. I can see his nose sniff gently, and I know he caught the scent of my arousal. Jesus, strike me dead now.

"You need a man," he says.

"It's been a long time." I look down and move to my own bag, working on it to avoid Conan's gaze. I'm so fucking mortified.

"Before you came into my office and said you'd be my bodyguard," I continue as I sift through my things for my toothbrush and face creams, "I had a life, you know. A secret one, but a life."

"There was a man?" Wait, was that an edge to his voice? I stop moving and look up at him standing like a statue in the dying twilight filtering through the white drapes. I lift my chin, deciding to give him the truth. I won't let my lust for him make a blabbering schoolgirl out of me.

"There were *men*. It's no secret to you or your brothers that back when the serpents ruled Darkwood Falls and forbade us women to see guys from other towns I'd go out on business and conferences and have one night stands."

He takes a step closer, the denim tightening over his powerful thighs. I watch him as he hunkers down, bringing his face close to mine, his scent causing a flare in my chest.

"And it's those one night stands that you miss?"

Now he's too close, smelling of virility and rustling fires.

"I miss the excitement, the adrenaline, the intimacy."

"Intimacy?" He cocks his scarred eyebrow. "What could be intimate about a one night stand? Intimacy is sharing yourself with another being, living with each other as one, in one body. In my book that's something you build up to."

"Well, what do you know." I cock an eyebrow back at him. "The big tough warrior teaching me a thing or two about relationships."

"Two of my werewolf brothers have known love, with your two best friends, and I have a line to their emotions. I can understand through their experiences, even if I don't feel the emotion myself. It's like when you tap into the emotions from a book."

I sit on the bed, now having the higher ground. I place my hands beside my naked thighs, the hem of my denim shorts biting a little into my flesh. I wish I'd worked out at least for a few days before I left Darkwood Falls with him. What was I thinking, Cote d'Azure, of course he would see more of my skin than back in the rainy woods that we come from.

"Then I guess I don't have to explain more. Ever since you came into my life you have been monitoring my every move, you have cameras in my room *and* my bathroom, and I couldn't even, you know, take care of myself at least."

"You could have told me when, and I would have given you some privacy."

"You mean I should have told you when I planned to masturbate, so you could make room for it in your schedule?" I burst into laughter, but Conan stares at me like he doesn't know what's funny.

"So what are you trying to tell me," he says when I manage to control my laughing. "That you'd like to go out and find a guy to hook up with?"

"Yes."

"That's out of the question."

Okay, this is my chance. I clear my throat and muster all the courage I can scrape together. "Then maybe you could, you know, scratch my itch." Blood fills my cheeks right after I've spoken out the words. I can't believe I've actually said it.

Conan stands slowly, dominating the room with every inch of his height. My grip on the edge of the bed tightens so much that my knuckles hurt.

"I understand your needs," he says in a far gentler tone than I expected. "I'm sure there are sex shops in Nice, we can go, you know, shopping, if you like."

"You mean like for a dildo?"

He nods and bends down to his bag, sifting through his neatly folded clothes. "You did the right thing, telling me. I am your bodyguard, and I do restrict you a lot, I'm aware of that. We should be able to discuss these things openly." He gives me a careful glance, as if choosing his words with care. "Like friends, if you want."

"Friends," I repeat. No, I want to cry out, I don't want to be your friend, I want to be your lover, I want you to crush me under that rocky body of yours on this five-star king size bed. Instead I let a smile quiver on my face and say, "Yes."

He smiles back, a clumsy smile. Maybe I'm the first person he's smiled for in a long time. I don't think I've seen him have fun before, even though I've heard him laugh in his room a few times with his brothers, or in Arianna's and Drago's kitchen during our dinners there.

Conan

I GET THE FEELING JANINE is more relaxed at dinner, but she still eats in silence, not looking at me. Ever since she and I met she's been tense, which is natural. I basically took over her life. Then she began feeling attracted to me, which made things more difficult for her. I understand better than she thinks.

"I hope you're not upset with me," I break the silence. "I didn't mean to be a jerk about, you know, it. It's just that—"

"You don't want to imprint on anyone, I get it," she says gently, then she looks at me for the first time since our talk up in the room. "But tell me. If I were a normal woman, not a Fated Female, would you sleep with me?"

The way she stares at me out of those intelligent cobalt blue eyes, the way her shiny blonde bob frames her heart-shaped face, it keeps my eyes glued to her. She's wearing pink lipstick that showcases the pretty shape of her lips with her delicate Cupid's bow, and her little black dress offers an enticing view into her cleavage.

I guess it's safe to admit at least to myself that I love the shape of Janine Kovesi's body. She's of medium height for most people but small for me even in her high heels, and has the delicate body of a dancer. She has thin, beautifully shaped legs, and delicate wrists and ankles, which are very much to my liking.

"I don't know what to say," I manage as I pull away from the emotions. "I haven't been a monk so far, and I don't intend to become one in the future but let me put it this way. I haven't been with a woman since I became your bodyguard. You've had my entire attention, and you will have it until both the threat of the serpents and of the other werewolf packs is eliminated."

"That might be a very long time."

Piano notes flow through the hotel restaurant, and romantic evening lights go on. We're on the terrace, the Mediterranean breeze wafting over. Fuck, the mood it puts me in, it's getting more difficult to resist thoughts of touching Janine.

"I guess. But believe me, I will do everything in my power to make sure you're as comfortable as possible that entire time."

"In case you haven't noticed in your long life, Mr. Wolf, we women are quite dependent on the good mood of our hormones. Tell me. If we get a dildo—together, at the sex shop—will that be my only companion until we've dealt with all the threats?"

Once again I don't know what to say.

"Besides." She resumes carefully cutting her food on her plate and stabbing small pieces with her fork. "Who is to say that after these threats are eliminated there won't be others?"

More threats means more time with Janine Kovesi. More time watching her, an idea that I find dangerously appealing.

"So what are you saying?" I start to pick at my food, too, avoiding her eyes. I don't know exactly what's happening to me, but I think I feel especially attracted to her, which is unsettling.

"I'm saying we'll need a long term solution, because I don't want to live as a nun. And I suppose you don't want to prolong this monkish lifestyle indefinitely either, do you?"

I glance at her over the table. The soft piano notes awaken my senses, mixing with the salty breeze and the scent that is natural to Janine Kovesi's body.

"I can deal with my needs."

"Of course. No one is watching *you* the entire time."

"Shouldn't we be discussing Lorenzo Piovra and possible strategies he might adopt instead? Making our plans? That's our pressing matter right now. We can talk about the rest when this is over."

"When we're back in Darkwood Falls?"

I bend to her over the table, my shoulders stiff. "We can visit the sex shop tomorrow right after the conference, if you like." A rush of excitement runs through me, and I don't want to think about why.

Her eyes pierce right through to the back of my skull. Damn it. This woman has power in her gaze that she's not even aware of. Of course men are intimidated by her.

"Any chance we might go tonight?"

I glance at my watch. "All stores are closed."

The way she looks at me, all that sass and hunger tell me this is another attempt to get me into some kind of arrangement. I lean back in my chair, focusing on the seafood on my plate.

"Why not just enjoy the evening as it is now? We're on the Cote d'Azure." I look around to make a point.

She follows my gaze, her eyes stopping on the first couple that's going to the dance floor. It's a young man and an older woman, obviously in love. He winds an arm around her waist, pulls her to him gently and rests his cheek against the top of her head. It's a gentle, loving gesture, and when he closes his eyes the chemistry of love is undeniable.

"Love is such a beautiful thing to watch," Janine says, eyes on the couple. "Especially the kind of love I've seen Arianna and Princess experience with Drago and Nero. Why wouldn't you want to experience that? Princess says it's the best thing that's ever happened to her, that it's an emotion worth dying for."

"That is exactly why I don't want to feel it. I am a protector, Miss Kovesi, that is my role within the pack. I must protect my brothers, see to the defense of the entire pack, see to the safety of the entire area and population of Darkwood Falls together with our werewolf brigade. I have to protect you. I can't afford to lose myself to love, or even desire."

"Drago and Nero have enemies, too. The serpents are still after them. Sullivan, the former mayor, has become a serpent himself and The Reaper's right hand. He's powerful, and he has a very personal grudge against Drago because he took Arianna away from him. As for Nero, should we even start on his long list of enemies?"

She fixes her intelligent eyes on mine, and I'm pulled to them like into a vortex. I can't rip my gaze away no matter what.

"You know what I think Conan, what I really think?" She leans over the table, exposing her cleavage. "I think you're just looking for excuses. You're big and powerful, the protector of the Wolf pack and the entire Darkwood Falls, but deep down you're a little boy that's scared of love. You feel the more people you love the weaker you are, and that may be something that will never change about you. In fact, I don't think you could change if you wanted to."

This would be the point where the girl throws her napkin on the table, pushes her chair back, and leaves the date, the patrons' eyes trailing after her. But Janine only leans back and places her hands on the chair's arms, keeping her eyes on me without even blinking. She's taking full responsibility for what she's just said, and she can't wait for me to challenge her.

But I'm too old and too experienced to give her satisfaction. No matter how smart Janine is, she's still a victim of young impulses. She wants a certain reaction from me, and her body chemistry is playing crazy to get it. But I won't be played with.

"You're right, Miss Kovesi," and pick up my wine.

Janine

I'M ALREADY UNDER THE covers in my bed when Conan emerges from the bathroom with only a towel around his waist, water drops glistening on those boulder-like muscles. I lick my lips, hating it that I desire him like this.

Under the covers I'm wearing my favorite black negligée. It makes my boobs look bigger than they are, and it's short enough to showcase my legs, which Princess says is always an advantage. As Conan lingers by the now open balcony windows, taking in the night sea breeze that makes for a romantic atmosphere paired with the music from the beach clubs, I push the covers aside. Clumsily, I remind myself that I am a strong, independent woman. I can go after what I want.

What in the world am I doing? He's half naked, with only a towel around his waist. My heart trembles inside my chest, my hands and knees, too, and my mouth goes dry. But there's no turning back now. I'm standing beside the bed, ready to prance over to him and touch his back. No, that would give him time to tell me no, maybe I should go straight for his dick, do something that will make him crave sex so much he won't be able to reject me.

I don't know who I'm trying to fool as I walk to him on shaky legs, my feet sinking into the thick soft rug, but he hears me anyway. He laughs softly.

He turns around, my heart leaping into my throat. He's now facing me, naked and wet, with only that flimsy towel around his waist. God, how I want to drop on my knees and take this beast's cock in my mouth, but no! I can't make a fool out of myself like that. Fuck, I shouldn't even want such a demeaning thing, what's wrong with me?

"Miss Kovesi," he says, a bit amused. "If you were trying to surprise me, may I remind you that I'm a werewolf. My hearing is so sharp that I can hear all the way down to the front office. Our good concierge is sound asleep in the manager's back office, by the way, I can hear him snore. And you think you can sneak up on me?"

"First of all, I wasn't sneaking." My voice trembles at first, but once I've gotten that first sentence out it's better. "I wasn't trying to surprise you. I was just, I don't know."

He stares hard at me, but not hard enough to make me desist. On the contrary, there's something in his gaze that invites me to go on. I take a couple of slow steps closer.

"How about we start by putting aside the formalities," I say. "We've known each other for a while, we've spent days and nights together, making plans, now we're even sharing a room. How about you start calling me Janine, and I'll call you Conan."

"That would bring intimacy between us. We're dangerously close already."

"What's dangerous about our closeness?" I stop just inches from him, feeling so small that he could crush me. Still, I keep my gaze locked on his, even though my heart is beating so fast it's gagging me.

"You're a Fated Female," he says. "Touching you could change things forever."

"And would that really be that bad?"

"Janine." God, the way he says my name, those big rough hands wrapping gently around my upper arms. My eyelids flutter shut as I let the sensation course all through my body. This feels so good it's incredible. Princess was right. Once a man like this touches you, you're lost.

"What you want from me isn't love or intimacy, Janine, it's sex." His voice is still soft as not to hurt my feelings, but I sense that behind the softness he relishes my burning shame. "But be honest with me and with yourself—would you take someone like me on your business meetings with your business partners? I'm not the sleek-haired boyfriend in an Armani suit that you always dreamt about. I'm not the guy you can show the world. I'm the kind of guy you fuck in secret, even *after* you've married the Armani-wearing bozo."

"That's not true," I breathe, my eyes filling with tears. I shouldn't have come on to him, I should have taken his first no for an answer.

"Even if that was different. I don't want to imprint on any woman, Janine, now or ever. I don't want to become like my brothers, puppies staring adoringly at their mistresses. I won't lose my head, become a slave to lust and need. I mean no offense to Arianna or Princess, I love them both, they became family the moment my brothers imprinted on them, but I don't want the same fate."

He looks deeply into my eyes one last time before he turns around, stepping out onto the balcony. I stay petrified in place, watching him leaning on the banister with his enormous back at me, a perfect muscular V-shape that narrows down to perfect buttocks and powerful legs. I swallow hard as I watch him, a statue of perfection overlooking the night lights of Cote d'Azure, the breeze carrying the beats and music from party yachts over to us.

As I'm standing here with my desire pulsing in me, rejected and hurting, I realize—Conan is enjoying it. He relishes the scent of my body chemistry that tells him how much into him I am, how much I want to feel him inside me even if only once. All of a sudden I'm transported back in time, when I had my first crush.

I was twelve, and he had eyes for every girl in school other than me. The more I chased him, sending him love notes—at first anonymous, then more and more desperate—the more he rejected me, and the more I wanted him. The same is happening now with Conan Wolf, but there's no way I'm going there again, no way I'm ever going to feel as desperate as I did back then. Spite and lust for vengeance replace the tears in my eyes. I will kill the desire I feel for Conan Wolf, or die trying.

CHAPTER III

Conan

Janine is about to take the stage. My senses are heightened to pick up Lorenzo Piovra's presence as soon as he sets foot on the hotel premises. And now that Janine is standing in her white business dress on the side of the stage, tablet in hand and ready to speak, I catch his scent. He steps into the conference room the moment Janine starts to talk.

I watch Lorenzo as he walks through the crowd, two werewolves of his pack flanking him on each side. He hasn't changed a bit since the last time I saw him—in the cave when I battled him for the Reaper's weapon, and won. He's the same young man with spiked dark hair like an Anime character, and freaky, pale blue eyes. He's got the eyes of a madman, and people tend to get out of his way because of it. He's tall and lean, but very powerful. Right now in his black Armani suit he looks just like... Fuck.

My eyes snap over to Janine, who's going about her business on the stage, without having noticed him. Had she caught sight of him, she surely would have stopped talking, because Lorenzo's eyes have that effect on everybody. But something else worries me right now—he's the exact type of man I described to her last night; the handsome guy in the Armani suit that could impress all her business partners, the kind of partner the entire world would approve of for a woman like her.

All I need to see is the way he looks at her, and I know—this is what he's playing at; he's going to seduce her. But then something else happens that throws me even more off—the more he watches Janine on stage and listens to her, the more he likes her; *genuinely*.

I spend the rest of the conference watching them, Janine moving gracefully on stage as she speaks, and Lorenzo sitting somewhere in the middle of the hall, staring at her. He's absorbed, and I can't blame him. The woman is the perfect blend between beauty and brilliance. There's something regal about her and, had she had freedom to live as a normal woman, I'm sure she would have married some duke by now. Women like her are rare, and aristocrats snatch them from the market quickly.

It hits me. If until yesterday the possibility of Janine and I coming together existed somewhere in the universe, it's dead now. I sensed the decision she made last night, I smelled it in her chemistry. Even though I was standing with my back at her, being a jerk in order to make her desist, I could feel her.

Yes, she is angry, which leaves the path open for Lorenzo. The more I think about it, the more my jaw clenches. She's a Fated Female, he's one of the most powerful werewolves alive, he could imprint on her.

Damn it. I didn't see *this* coming.

I hurry to her side so that I'm right behind her when they finally come face to face. Luckily there are people who make it over to her with questions before Lorenzo does—he's actually taking his time in a corner with his bodyguards—and I get to show him to her.

"I noticed him," she whispers over her shoulder as she gives autographs on 'Make Your Hobby Your Career' books that people come to her with. "He has striking eyes, I couldn't miss him."

Are you attracted to those eyes? Is what I want to ask, but I clench my jaw and get a grip.

"He might have come here with the purpose of imprinting on you."

"Oh, really? That means I could actually get laid soon."

"This isn't funny." I manage to keep my cool on the outside, but fear nestles in my chest. He could indeed use her sex starvation to his advantage.

I grab Janine's shoulders and turn her around, looking deep into her eyes, my mouth close to hers as I tell her this. "Janine, listen to me. You are a brilliant woman, but Lorenzo is a very old werewolf, and no matter how high an IQ you have you're no match for him. He's going to try and play on your need for affection, for intimacy, for sex. You have to keep a cool head, no matter what."

"I guess it would have helped if another werewolf had imprinted on me by now, wouldn't it?"

But I don't get to answer because Lorenzo and his bodyguards are already here.

"Miss Kovesi," he addresses her, his voice musical and pleasant. Accommodating, seductive. Fuck, bastard's good.

"Lord Piovra." She offers him a friendly smile, like a lady, holding out her hand. So far so good, at least she's not acting like a flattered giggly schoolgirl.

He takes her hand and kisses it while keeping his pale blue eyes on her face. Any other woman would be sighing already, at least inwardly but, to my surprise, Janine doesn't seem very impressed. Probably because she's used to good-looking werewolves by now, and Piovra's dashing good looks can't strike her as hard as they would if he were the first supernatural she ever met.

But Piovra is determined to get through to her, and he continues to stare at her in a way that makes me want to split his jaw.

"I was impressed by your talk. Encouraging women to become entrepreneurs, that's as virtuous as environmental work if you ask me."

"Then too bad you're not ruling a government or two around the world. Your country would be all green and full of happy women," Janine replies without losing her composure, the polite smile still on her lips. Once again I'm impressed—Lorenzo can't even flatter her into loosening up.

Janine motions to me with her hand. "I understand you've already met my companion, Mr. Conan Wolf."

"Companion," Lorenzo says, his eyes meeting mine for the first time in two centuries. "I thought he was your bodyguard."

"Oh?" Janine frowns at him, feigning ignorance. "And where did you get that information?"

The glint in Lorenzo's eyes betrays that he's busted. Janine's smarts cut right through. Indeed, he couldn't have known, not unless he had spies in Darkwood Falls.

"The way he stared at you from the shadows the entire conference," he says. "He looked like a man with a job—or an obsession."

Janine smiles back at Lorenzo. "And since the second possibility is out of the question…"

No one reacts for a few moments that feel like an eternity, but then Janine breaks the silence, straightening her back and hooking an arm elegantly around Lorenzo's. He's not an easy man to read, but I can tell he likes her bold yet classy manner as she leads him out of the conference room, his bodyguards and me following.

"I'm glad you agreed to meet me a few days early. That way we can enjoy together the Cote d'Azure while we talk business," she says as we take our seats in the VIP section of the hotel lobby.

"Actually, the business we need to discuss is of a very delicate nature," Lorenzo says. "There are things I need to show you, things can't be simply—" He leans towards her, his blue eyes set on her. "Told."

"You can at least tell me what it's about, I'm sure." Janine signals the waiter like a woman in charge, which gives Lorenzo pause. My cheek twitches as I suppress a smile. Lord Piovra is in for quite a few surprises with Janine Kovesi.

"There are too many people listening."

Janine looks at me. "Conan. Would you mind taking Lord Piovra's boys for a drink at the hotel bar?"

"I can't leave your side, and you know it," I grunt.

"I'm sure Lord Piovra isn't here to hurt me. If he were, he would have insisted that we met in Venice at his palace, where we couldn't have done much about it."

"There's no place where I can't do *something* about it," I say through my teeth. "Provided that I remain by your side."

"Please, Conan." She puts her small hand over mine, and electricity runs through my skin. I make a conscious effort not to shudder. Turns out the lightest touch of a Fated Female is enough to do a werewolf some damage.

"I'll tell you what. I'll take the boys to the other side of the lobby—it's big enough, and full. That way I can keep an eye on you."

I turn my back and do it without waiting for an answer, but perk up my ears to hear everything they talk about from a distance. I watch from the shadows as they warm up to each other, watching for little signs in Janine's attitude that would betray if she loosens up towards him. To my relief she doesn't, but then he invites her for a walk on the famous promenade.

And who would refuse a walk to remember on the Promenade des Anglais. Janine has a soft spot for history, and I can sniff out the delight in her as Lorenzo tells her stories, helping her picture what life used to be like on the promenade of Nice centuries ago. He would know, wouldn't he?

Lorenzo's bodyguards and I follow them close behind, close enough to smell and hear them without much effort. Damn it, I could be even closer if not for all the attention I'm drawing. They might as well have an elephant trailing them.

While the two werewolves manage to stay inconspicuous in the crowd, I'm too big and mean-looking to go unnoticed. I swear under my breath. I can keep in the shadows under different circumstances, but not while the woman I protect is walking on the overcrowded Nice promenade on the arm of the very man I'm trying to protect her from.

But I can't resist. I get really close behind them, Lorenzo's bodyguards on my heels, ready to intervene if I did something unexpected. Not that it would help them. They pose no danger to me, and they know it.

I keep my ears perked up for the conversation between Janine and Lorenzo. He keeps trying to charm her but she forces him to get to the point, which fills my heart with this feeling that has been growing inside of me ever since I met her. The woman can hold her ground and, to be honest, I'm impressed that she can keep such a cool head with someone like Lorenzo. The women I know go giggly and often lose their heads for werewolves, because werewolves are compelling to humans, just like vampires. Perhaps Janine is resilient because her two best friends are mated to werewolves, and she's already into me?

Or is she over me already? I hurt her badly last night, I offended her, knowing full well what I was doing. I tried to push her away once and for all, but that might just have been the worst move I've ever made.

We're getting closer to the hotel where Janine and I are staying, which cuts Lorenzo's time with her short. He decides to make it clear why he wanted to meet her of all people as they turn to each other in front of the hotel.

"I can save Darkwood Falls from the serpents, and even send The Reaper to his maker forever. But for that I need *you*, Janine."

"Why me?"

"I wish things were so simple and I could just *tell* you the reason. But that's why I say there are things that can't be *told*, I have to *show* them to you." He kisses her small white hand with the slightly curved, long fingernails. I imagine those fingernails scratching their way down my back, leaving trails of blood in their wake as punishment for the way I treated her.

"Before you go," Janine stops him. "One more thing I'm just *dying* to know. How come your invitation reached me on the very day that Conan Wolf became my bodyguard? And how did you know he was my protector? No one here knew that, actually nobody outside our closest circle in Darkwood Falls."

He smiles full of secrets and straightens his back, looking even taller. "I'm sure you have a lot of questions, and I'll be happy to answer all of them at my palace in Venice."

I should be analyzing every word this bastard says, putting it through the filter of my analytical mind, but I can't. All I can think about is what a great couple they'd make, and it makes me want to beat him to a pulp right here, in front of her. Lorenzo is a tall, pretty-face werewolf, looking dashing in a suit, while Janine an elegant business-woman with intelligence oozing out of her eyes and sassiness out of her entire attitude. Lorenzo is exactly the type she's been looking for all her life.

A black car pulls up at the curb in front of the hotel, and Lorenzo gives us both a nod as one of his bodyguards holds the door open for him.

"I'm looking forward to your visit," he says before the black door thuds shut, and the bodyguards walk to the other side of the car. Janine watches them drive away.

Conan

JANINE SEEMS LOST IN a daydream as she enters the room. She kicks off her pumps, and her entire body language changes. She's relaxed, as if she's either by herself or with someone who doesn't make her nervous or self-conscious at all.

There's a bucket of ice on the table, and a bottle of Moet in it—VIP treatment for conference speakers. Janine pours herself a flute of cool champagne, glancing briefly at me.

"Want one?"

"No, thank you."

"Another no drinking no sinning member of the Wolf pack. Was Drago the only decadent one?"

"Achilles is, too. But the rest of us prefer to keep a somber reserve. Sorry you got stuck with me and not with one of my more joyous brothers."

Janine ignores my stinging remark and walks to the open windows, running her fingers through her hair. Her moves are so natural, and at the same time elegant.

"What do you make of what happened tonight, Conan?" she says over her shoulder, leaning on the window frame and staring out at the sea in the rapidly darkening dusk, lights already turning on in distant buildings.

"You were the one arm in arm with him. You tell me." Fuck, I can't keep the edge out of my voice.

"Yes, but you're the one who can smell people's body chemistry, you can assess his intentions."

"I think he wants to imprint on you," I spit that out like it's poison on my tongue.

Janine turns around, the flute of champagne in her hand. "Where did that come from?"

My jaw ticks. "You asked me what his body chemistry said. That is what I picked up."

She snorts like she believes I'm making fun of her. "You know, Conan, I admit I'm super curious about what makes me so special that Lorenzo invited me of all people to his palace in Venice, considering he's such a powerful werewolf and all. But do you know *why* I'm so curious? Because I never felt special before, and I can't imagine actually being it. Now a new blast hits me, namely that this powerful werewolf who's been alive for centuries and basically owns all of Europe wants to imprint on me. It doesn't make any sense."

"It will make sense soon enough. We're going to his palace tomorrow, and I might be able to put two and two together with only a few details more than what we have right now. You might not need to keep his company for long."

Janine leans with her back against the window, cradling her glass and looking at me like she's calculating something in her mind, a cute line between her furrowed eyebrows.

"Maybe it wouldn't be such a bad idea, him imprinting on me."

"Oh. Thinking about switching sides to the Piovras?"

"How quick you are to think ill of me." She walks over as she speaks. "I was thinking of eliminating the Piovras, actually. Not in *that* way," she reacts to the look on my face. "But make them cease and desist, leave Darkwood Falls in your hands."

"And what makes you think that Lorenzo would give up Darkwood Falls if he imprinted on you?"

"Because, like you said, when a werewolf imprints he becomes an adoring puppy for the woman he imprinted on. Drago and Nero don't spare any effort to fulfill Arianna and Princess's every wish. Maybe Lorenzo will be the same with me."

"Not maybe, he'd surely. Every werewolf who's imprinted on a woman can't breathe without her, and can't bear to see anything but happiness in her face."

"So he would do anything for me, right?"

"Yes, but you forget one very important thing—you'd do the same for him. So what if he asks you to betray the Wolf pack, tell him all the secrets you know? Trust me, when a werewolf imprints, the woman becomes high on him, addicted to him. He oozes pheromones and an emotional appeal that makes him irresistible to her."

"Oh, I know that." There's defiance in her face. "I know how Arianna and Princess love their werewolves. You say you don't want to become an 'adoring puppy' like your brothers, but believe me, I don't want to become the love struck schoolgirl that Arianna and Princess have become either."

She downs the champagne and licks it off her thin but beautifully shaped lips, then points at me with the index of the hand in which she holds the flute. She moves like a mafia queen, delicate, but powerful.

"So you're saying I shouldn't entertain the idea of giving myself to Lorenzo. Very well. Then how do you suggest that I keep him at bay while I'm at his palace in Venice? Because I don't think he's the kind of man that will let me leave until he's achieved his purpose."

"No, Lorenzo isn't the kind of man who gives up."

"He's also a man of many mysteries. He left many open questions to ensure that we join him at his palace in Venice. He's yet to tell us in what way I'm special, why he can only beat The Reaper with my help, how he knew that you were my bodyguard and how his invitation happened to reach me on the very day you became my protector. Lorenzo has worked his spell, making me look forward to his answers in Venice, but I have one question, Conan, that only you can answer."

She's now so close that I can feel her breath on my chest, right between my pecs, between the upper buttons of my shirt. "How are we gonna get out of there if we find ourselves trapped?"

"That's not a question of *if*. Lorenzo will try to keep us, that's for sure—you as his mated wife, and me... He won't let me leave his palace still carrying the Reaper's secret weapon. He'll either fight me for it, or demand that I give it to him."

"Because it can only be earned or given," she whispers, remembering the story. "What is that weapon, Conan?"

"I can't tell you that. Only Lorenzo and I know that, and we'll both take it to the grave."

"Why the secret?"

"You saw the Lord of the Rings, I trust?"

"I read the books."

What did I expect? "Well, the Reaper's secret weapon is very much like the Ring of Power. It corrupts people. It makes them destroy each other and, finally, the world around them. It takes a special kind of resilience to master the weapon."

"That a man like you should watch Lord of the Rings."

"I didn't. Like you, I read the books. It intrigued me how Tolkien knew the Elvish languages. They're real languages, you know."

Her intelligent eyes glint. "I thought he invented them."

"People assumed he did because of his extensive notes, but he was studying and analyzing the languages, not inventing them. At least that's what he was unconsciously doing."

"Fascinating. And how did he have access to the knowledge? Secret documents?"

I have to repress a smile that would have come out warm and accommodating. I love how she hungers for information, and how she twists it in her pretty head.

"Not only that. I think he had psychic access to long lost knowledge, but that's not what we're here to investigate. We're here for other secrets."

She turns from me, trying to hide her feelings, but I already smelled it in her chemistry. She's losing control over her attraction to me.

"True," she says. "But before we embark on this journey we should both be ready. There is something I need to solve before we venture between the dangerous walls of Lorenzo's palace."

She places the flute on the table by the open window, and pours herself another.

"Would you mind?" She offers me her back, inviting me to unzip her dress. I was the one to zip it up this morning, so it seems harmless—at first.

I slide her zipper down, revealing more and more of her white skin. She's slightly freckled, which adds to her special femininity.

I take a step back when I'm done, but I can't take my eyes off of her. I can't help but watch as she pushes the dress off her shoulders and lets it pool at her feet, stepping out of it. I lick my hard lips without thinking. What a sight she is. She's wearing red lace underwear, her shiny blonde bob shimmering in the Mediterranean lights. The breeze mixes with Janine's natural ocean scent, but I can tell the difference quite well. Then, without even trying, I find the words for her—an ocean nymph.

Yes, the scent of her essence as a Fated Female, oozing out of her more and more in the presence of a werewolf. Actually, tonight two werewolves have been interested in her, Lorenzo and me, which lends her Fated Female energy even more power.

I hope that her pride will keep her from trying anything, and that she'll just head to the bathroom without noticing how my jeans have tightened over the aching swell under my belt. But what she does is turn around, facing me in full, dressed only in red lace bra and panties.

I can't help staring at her, drinking in the elegant shape of her body. A body that could so easily be crushed, while her personality could crush the world. Fuck, I have to back off before she comes on to me, because I won't be able to resist her this time, and I'm dangerous when I'm horny.

"What are you doing, Janine?" I grunt through my teeth, glaring at her. I have to scare her off before it's too late.

"I'll be blunt, Conan, because we're not exactly spoilt for time. I need to be with a man, or to find relief some other way, and it has to be tonight, because otherwise I might fall victim to Lorenzo's advances. He is a very attractive man, and I'm sex starved."

"You find him attractive?"

One corner of her mouth quirks up, sass filling her heart-shaped face. "What human woman wouldn't? All werewolves are insanely attractive to us."

"I try not to be."

"You try and you fail." She walks over, her essence and her scent engulfing me. "You have a brutish face, and muscles that show what a powerful, hardcore beast you are. Your masculine essence could drive any woman crazy. Today at the conference you kept in the shadows, protecting me, but when you walked into the light, standing by my side when Lorenzo came, didn't you notice how women stared at you?" She creams between her legs, and I can smell it. I clench my fists so hard I feel my knuckles protrude. No matter what, I have to hold my ground.

"They basically licked you all over with their eyes." Her voice is low, fluid, her eyes falling to my lips. She raises her hand, touching them. Her arousal creams her panties, and my cock strains angrily against my jeans. I should push her away, right now, but I just can't find the strength to do it. Her touch, the warmth of her delicate body so close to mine, I can't rip myself away.

"You know what I think, Conan? I think you enjoy making women horny for you, giving them wet dreams, making them crave you. You know you're an irresistible beast, and it gives you pleasure to mess with women's heads."

"It's true." I keep my voice low, but it's deep and vibrant in my chest. It makes her pupils widen, probably because it adds to the animal sex appeal she just talked about. "But I wasn't messing with your head yesterday, if that's what you think. I wasn't trying to hurt you."

"Oh, no? Swear to me that you didn't enjoy turning your back on me and feeling my hungry eyes graze up and down your body. You have sharp senses, you surely smelled my arousal. Swear to me you didn't relish knowing I wanted you so baldy that it hurt, and treating me like I wasn't even interesting enough to stir your cock."

"You don't understand," I say gruffly. "I can't afford to get horny around you. It's dangerous."

"Yes, dangerous because you don't want to imprint on me." She waves her hand in a dismissive gesture. The same hand with which she just touched my lips. Thankfully she doesn't notice that I lean my head towards her, yearning for her touch back on my mouth that feels dry now. I'm inexplicably thirsty.

"Suppose I imprinted on you. Tonight. That would be a deal-breaker for Lorenzo. He hopes you'll agree to a union with him, that's his price for giving you answers. When he met you today you were still free, untouched by a werewolf. One kiss between you and me, and that could change. He'd take it as a personal insult if you went to him in Venice with your bodyguard-slash-mate. He'd know whatever happened between us happened right after you met him, and he could even drop this façade of good guy, and go into a frontal attack. Because there's nothing good or gentle about his true face, believe me."

"Oh, I do believe you. I've met plenty of men with masks. One glance in Lorenzo's eyes was enough to know he was faking good nature. He's a villain."

It's like an iron fist has let go of my heart. "I'm glad to see you can't be seduced by a good façade."

"There was a time when I could be fooled. No longer." Hardness of character adds to the sass in her voice. "And you can't fool me either. You would do and say anything to dissuade me from coming on to you, but you don't have to worry. I won't hit on you again in my life, I swear it."

She walks backwards away from me. "But I do want your help with this."

She turns to the side table next to her bed and calls the front office. "Do you have what I asked for?" She gives the device a satisfied smile, which can only mean she got an affirmative answer. "Please bring it up."

She hangs up and stares me in the face like she's got a wicked plan.

"Conan, you and I are going to pull off our plans with Lorenzo Piovra. But for that I need you to do something for me tonight. I promise you, it's not imprinting, and I won't let that happen even if things become smoldering hot."

I frown. "Smoldering hot?"

"Just promise me you'll help me with this."

"I can't promise anything if I don't know what I'm promising."

"Just do it, blindly, and in return I promise that I'll do anything you ask of me at Lorenzo's palace, anything that will benefit the Wolf pack."

I hesitate.

"This might not seem like a very valuable promise right now," Janine says. "But just consider how much Lorenzo wants to imprint on me."

Indeed, at this moment the game is entirely in Janine's hands. I guess she can't ask me for the world, can she. And she already said it's not about imprinting, so I nod. "I promise."

Janine's cobalt blue eyes fill with darkness, her smile mischievous. "Thank you."

CHAPTER IV

Janine

On my request, Conan opens the door after the knock, and the concierge hands him the box with my order. Due to Lorenzo's visit, Conan and I didn't get to go shopping, so I had the concierge do the dirty work for me.

Anticipation swirls in my stomach. I can't wait to see Conan's face when he opens the box and unwraps the paper from the present I got myself. The exchange of looks between him and the concierge sends a prickle through my stomach—Conan still has no idea what's gonna go down in this room tonight, but the concierge does, because he knows what he bought for me.

He glances from Conan to me—I walk up and press my body to the side of the huge man in the white shirt that almost snaps on his big arm muscles, my small hand gripping his bicep. The concierge's drooping eyes widen, since I'm wearing only my red lace underwear and the look of a woman who's just about to get it on wildly with this guy.

"Tip the man, Conan," I say in a sexy voice. "It was a special job that I asked him to do for me."

Conan pushes bills in the man's hand, eager to get rid of him and be alone with me again to demand answers. He slams the door in the man's face and turns to me, his eyes glinting blood red.

"What the hell was that?" he demands. I take the box from his hands, staring him in the eye, then turn around and walk to the bed with it.

This is it. I'm about to set my plan for revenge in motion. It can go two ways. It could torment him and make him want me like he never wanted a woman in his life, or I could lose his respect forever, and have to endure his contemptuous looks for the rest of my life.

I open the lid and begin unpacking the order.

"I asked you a question, Janine."

I press my eyes shut—I like the way he said that. Like a boss, like the man of the house. I pick up the item and turn around, stroking it up and down as I explain.

"We talked about dildos last night, didn't we?"

"Yes, but...."

He's lost for words, which makes me feel slightly more confident. My blood still runs like crazy through my veins, but at least I threw Conan off. He looks at me with an open mouth for the first time in days, watching me as I stroke the big, veined replica of a cock.

"As I said, I need sexual relief before we enter Lorenzo's palace for God knows how long. There might be eyes everywhere, so this may be my last chance. If I had little privacy under your watch, I might have none under Lorenzo's."

"I see." Conan licks his hard masculine lips, a gesture that makes my blood rush. "Then I shall give you some right now."

He turns to the door but I stop him. "I want you to watch."

He stops in place, his white shirt tightening over the tense muscles in his back.

"You can't be serious." There's genuine surprise in his voice, not the anger I expected. He keeps his back to me, so unfortunately I can't see his face.

I sit on the bed, crossing my legs.

"I have been dreaming about you for a long time, Conan. Probably since the day I met you. The least you can do for me is let me look at you while I do myself, and watch me in return. Come on, it's merely small pleasures that I'm asking for, isn't it?"

He turns to look at me, and I see something in his eyes that wasn't there before. "You don't understand, Janine. I wouldn't be able to give you what you want even if things were different."

"Why not?" I can't believe the entitlement in my attitude. Sitting here on the bed, legs crossed, demanding answers like a queen with a dildo in her lap.

"Because I'm not normal that way. I don't want what normal men want."

"You're into kinks?"

"Kinks." He snorts. "I've been a soldier all my life, fought many wars, I've seen and lived things that changed me forever. I cannot see women and relationships like normal men do." He walks to me as he talks.

"I never felt anything tender or sweet for a woman. I used women, and it wasn't the vanilla kind of using."

"Why don't you tell me more about that." I set the dildo aside on the bed, my hand slipping into my panties. My legs are still crossed so that Conan doesn't get a good look at what I'm doing, but his eyes drop down my lap. Hell, I don't even know where I'm getting the guts from to even do this right now, but the booze is helping.

"Janine, I shouldn't be anywhere near you right now."

"You promised you would help me. And this is what I wanted your help with—cumming."

He balls his fists, his knuckles protruding white. His jaw ticks, his irises glinting blood red.

"You said—"

"I said it would be imprinting-safe. And it will be."

"But you want to have sex with me."

"Oh, no, no, no, my handsome beast. I wanted to have sex with you last night, when you treated me like dirt. You think your imprinting on a woman is such a big deal, but let me remind you that giving her heart forever is a huge deal for a woman as well. I was ready to fall in love with you yesterday, give myself to you forever, but now I'm light years away from such intentions."

My hand moves faster in my panties as I tell him that, the lust for revenge fueling me.

"I want you to watch me as I pleasure myself," I say in a worked up voice. "If things go really well, I may ask you to touch me. But you won't imprint on me because, as you said, for that you would have to kiss me or fuck me. None of that is going to happen."

Conan doesn't say anything, he just stands there staring at me as I masturbate and talk to him at the same time. I'm so turned on that I arch my body as I speak, my tone and breath changing, my thighs squirming. I'm still wearing my high heels, and I decide I won't be taking them off tonight. I'll make this fabulous beast curse the moment he turned his back on me, being a jerk.

"The first thing you will delight me with is this—talk to me about all the dirty ways you'd take me. Maybe we can't share much physical intimacy, but how about some dirty secrets. You can't imprint on me by doing that."

"Why, Janine?" he breathes. "Why do you provoke me like this?"

"Provoke you? You didn't seem interested in me at all last night, I figured there's nothing I can do to turn you on. After all, you're an old soul, a soldier who's seen it all, a crazy sexy specimen that women throw themselves at. Let's just say I want to use you in my own perverted way."

"You don't understand. You put yourself in danger."

"Are you going to hurt me?"

"Not physically."

"Then no more trying to talk me out of this. Keep your promise, and I will keep mine in return—I'll do whatever you ask of me in Venice. I'll do everything in my power for the Wolf pack to win, and nothing will ever change my allegiance. Tell me the dark and dirty things you're into."

He hesitates. Maybe I should give him some incentive. I lift my feet from the ground, feeling grateful for my natural flexibility, and slide the panties down my legs. I bring my feet back down, and open my legs for Conan to see my now slick pussy.

He looks away, but I won't let him. He'll have to take all of this, I'll have him crave me like I'm the only woman left on earth.

"No, Conan. I want you to keep your eyes on me all the time."

I grab the dildo and his lips part, fire in his eyes.

"Please, don't," he whispers. I grin, noticing his hard-on through his pants. It must hurt.

I push the tip of the dildo inside of me, inhaling sharply as the hard thing parts my walls. It's been so long. "Tell me, Conan. What do you like doing to women?"

"I like only a certain type of woman."

"Oh, this is interesting. What kind?"

"Bad girls. Women who've done harm, who've broken hearts. Who've taken their girlfriends' men, who broke up marriages, who suck every cock with a yacht they can get their surgically pumped-up lips on."

My lust is starting to leave me, and Conan notices. He grins, understanding that the tables have turned, and he could actually win this one. He moves closer to me, and I feel the need to cover myself, but I manage to resist the urge and not give him satisfaction.

"I'm a hard man, Janine, not just in body and spirit, but in everything that I am. The hardness you see in my face, it's there for a reason. But since we're here." He hunkers down, but he's so big that only brings him face to face with me. "I'll make a confession. I've imagined those pretty lips of yours wrapped around my cock, your intelligent eyes looking up at me like you worshipped me while you sucked me off."

I swallow hard. This makes me feel naked and vulnerable. Damn, he's winning.

"That was the closest thing I ever felt to something tender." He juts out his chin. "Now are you sure you want to go through with this?"

No, I won't let him humiliate me by making me feel vulnerable and weak. I force myself to smile, and touch his hand. I have this one chance of turning the tables in my favor again, and I'll sure as hell take it. I guide his hand to the dildo.

"You do it. Pump me with it, slowly, and tell me more of how you fucked those women. Do you only fuck their mouths, or do you occasionally take their pussies, too?"

God, the delight at seeing this brute's scarred but handsome face flooded with surprise. He doesn't move the hand with the dildo, so I plant my feet still in high heels on each side and move slowly against the dildo, rocking my hips down its length until it fills me.

"Oh, God," I whisper as my inside clenches full of pleasure around the fake cock. The experience is amazing because I get to do this looking straight into Conan's face, actually feeling like I'm doing him. I don't know if it's only because he's a werewolf, and therefore special, but I've never been so attracted to anyone before.

A darkness falls over his eyes, and I realize he must be starting to enjoy seeing me like this, worked up, all sweaty and flushed and almost spilling my juices over a fake cock with my hungry eyes on him. And he's not even doing anything for it. I have to take my power back.

"You do it, too," I command, panting. "Take your cock out and jerk off. I want to see you."

"But...."

"No buts. You promised. I'm the boss tonight, you do what I tell you. And you get to tell me what to do in Venice."

My request takes him aback, I can see that, but the darkness remains in his eyes, which can only mean he's going to do it. He takes his free hand to his jeans, and I'm lost.

I lick my hot lips as I watch him unbuckle his belt and whip his cock out. I breathe in sharply as it springs free, big and veined, its big head purple with need. He wanted this as badly as I did while I was sliding up and down the dildo in his hand.

He wraps his large fist around his cock, his strong knuckles showing white. He strokes himself hard as I use the dildo, his burning eyes unwavering from my face. I'm pulled into them, unable to look away. His irises look like those of a dragon, like lava. I've never seen anything like it before. He's taking me, owning me with those eyes as he puts one knee on the bed between my legs, standing over me as he jerks off.

The muscles in his arm snake under his white shirt as he works on himself, his hard lips parted, his face a beautiful bronze hue apart from the scar running down from his eyebrow to his upper lip, a steady white reminder of the violence he's used to.

"If I were one of those women," I say as I'm close to cumming. "What would you do to me now? How would you take me?"

"I'd straddle your face," he says in his deep voice, now gruff with need. Just looking at the pleasure in his face is enough to bring me to the verge of cumming. "And have you lick my balls. Then I'd twist my hand in your hair and push my cock deep into your mouth, down your throat until you choked on it. Depending on your sins, on what people you'd crossed and how vile you were, I'd spill my cum all over your face, making you aware of how you're sucking off a man you'd never introduce to your high society friends. But you, Janine." His bad boy gaze changes, his irises like lava gaining a different kind of intensity.

"I would never do any of those things to you, not like that. I feel very differently about you."

"How," I manage hungrily. "How do you feel about me?"

"I..." But I can't hear what he says because the way he looks at me makes me explode around the dildo, coating it in the essence of my pleasure. I push my head back into the fluffy duvet, my eyes rolling as the orgasm runs through me. The idea that I'm being taken by the magnificent Conan Wolf shakes me to the very marrow of my bones.

I come back to myself and look up into his eyes. God, the hunger with which he's watching me penetrates my entire body.

"Where do you want it?" he asks.

"What?"

"I'm cumming, Janine. Damn it, I can't hold it for long, where do you want it?"

I take my hand to my cheek. "Here."

Conan pushes himself up on his knee that's still between my legs, bringing that big cock sticking out of his fly to my face. The scent of him, of horny man, envelops me.

"Are you sure?" he says huskily, the purple head of his cock close to my lips, but not touching them. One touch could be enough to trigger imprinting, and I understand that he doesn't want to risk it, but still. I wish he would, so badly.

His warm cum splashes my cheek, the sexiest sound filling my ears at the same time—him, moaning. A deep but vulnerable moan like an animal being hurt. I can't stop staring up at him, taking in the scene, a scene that I'll remember for the rest of my life.

I'm still not sure what hit me as Conan drops to his knees on the floor. I come slowly up to a sitting position, my legs trembling from the way I worked myself against the dildo and the orgasm it gave me while I watched Conan's face. Now he's on his knees in front of me, looking down, and all I can see is the dark crown of his head.

I watch him breathe hard, his muscular shoulders moving up and down, the jeans stretching over those thighs that could smash rocks.

"Forgive me." His voice sends a shiver down my back. He sounds regretful, almost broken. "I shouldn't have used you like that."

"I asked you to," I whisper.

Conan looks up at me, and I can see he's feeling guilty.

"I wish," he says, "I wish I could kiss you. I wish I could take your face between my hands, lay you on your back and kiss your lips, your neck, and your breasts, and the inside of your thighs, if that way I could make up for this." He looks around as if what we just did was an act of sacrilege.

To make up for this... That's the only reason why he'd do it. Not because he wants me, or because he's falling for me like I am for him, hopelessly.

"What exactly is it that you regret," I hiss through my teeth. I'm so frustrated that I grip the duvet with both hands, hoping he doesn't notice it. "That you had to let yourself be dragged into this, or that your cum is dripping off my face?"

"Both," he replies without hesitation. "This should have never happened between us, much less this way. I shouldn't have used you."

Used me. That's all it was to him.

I stick out my chin. "Seems your memory is playing tricks on you. I was the one using you, Conan. Remember?"

He doesn't say anything, which only fuels my spite, the hurt now consuming me.

"You liked taking me in this dirty way, and you better own it. Because I'm not going to deny this is the way I wanted it. But you know what? I won't fall madly in love with you, so relax. And I will never give you my body either."

Conan

THE GONDOLIER STANDS behind me, pushing us slowly through the dark and murky canal into what seems to be Lorenzo's Venice water driveaway. It's chilly, the walls of his historical family estate rising from the dark water.

I have three plans ready for getting Janine out of here alive and unscathed if things go south, and I'd normally feel confident about them. But this is Lorenzo Piovra and his pack that I'm up against, the Italian mafia of the werewolf world. They can be cruel and bloody despite the good-guys façade they put up for Janine. But that's not even what worries me most.

I'm worried about her in ways that make me feel vulnerable like I never felt before. When the hell did I get emotionally involved? I didn't imprint on her, I'm sure about that. Deep down I'm also worried that Lorenzo will win her over, and it has nothing to do with the pack's safety. It has to do with the cocktail of feelings bubbling up inside of me for the woman, and my primal instinct to make her mine. We didn't go all the way last time, and that haunts me.

I get off the gondola directly onto Lorenzo's granite patio, holding out my hand for Janine. I know Lorenzo would have liked to help her off himself, but I keep too close to her, making it awkward for him to even try.

Janine puts her small white hand into mine, allowing me to pull her onto solid ground. How very unfit we are for each other, aren't we? We're so different, people feel compelled to stare wherever we turn up together, like they stared a few nights ago at the hotel terrace restaurant. My hand looks like a large rough paw compared to her unblemished porcelain hand. She's so delicate and feminine it seems almost a sacrilege to see her by the side of a brute, like me.

"Welcome," Lorenzo says, his musical voice bouncing off the stone walls when the three of us come face to face. "To my home. This palazzo has belonged to my family for hundreds of years," he explains as he leads us inside, flanking Janine on her left while I walk alongside her on the right. Only a few of his men trail us, but I can feel the eyes watching from shadowy archways and from behind pillars.

We're soon inside a dark and chilly main hall that, I must admit, has some serious charm. Janine is fascinated, I can smell it and see it. Her lips are slightly parted as she gawks at our surroundings, absorbed by Lorenzo's story, a story that I stop listening to. I can't help stealing glances at her, she's so compelling she enraptures me.

I keep staring at her mouth, wondering what it would have felt like to push my cock between those nicely shaped lips. She's wearing transparent lip-gloss that enhances their size. I've been around her for some time now, and I know she's unhappy with them because they're thin. If she only knew she has the prettiest mouth I've ever seen.

Obviously I'm not the only one with that opinion. I mean look how that jackass Lorenzo stares at her mouth as well. He must be thinking about fucking it. I clench my fist. I swear I'm gonna split his jaw before I leave here.

Janine shivers as we head deeper into the dark but fascinating palazzo with its long labyrinthic halls. I shrug off my jacket and whirl it around her shoulders, rubbing her arms over the sleeves to drive her body heat up. But is that really all I want? Or am I taking advantage of the situation to put my hands on her?

"The rooms are prepared for you," Lorenzo says. "Mr. Wolf, yours is right next to Janine's, I imagined you'd want it that way. I must warn you there won't be much privacy here because, well, you, Mr. Wolf will understand. The pack Piovra have a reputation, security matters."

"I understand you mean there are surveillance cameras, Lorenzo," I say with grit in my voice. "But I don't see in what way Janine could be dangerous to your pack from inside her room. I understand why you want to have *me* monitored, but her? Besides, that's no way to treat a guest."

Lorenzo's jaw tightens. "You're right, maybe I should have the cameras removed from Janine's room. But I'll do it only because you're special, Janine. I wouldn't do it for just anyone."

"Come on," Janine puts in with fake sweetness. "I can't possibly be a danger to you, so I'll hardly take that as a favor."

The mask of noble generosity vanishes from Lorenzo's face, and my cock twitches as she displays her smarts.

"I'm purely human," she adds, "with only one werewolf to protect me from an entire pack if things go nasty. What could I possibly do against you from a guest room in your palazzo?"

"Well," Lorenzo says with a slimy smile, "that one werewolf protecting you is one of the deadliest men in the world."

"You said it yourself—*one*. Do you honestly think he could take down your entire pack?" She motions around at the walls and shadows as if she knows what lurks behind them. She keeps that sassy smile on her face, which makes it hard as hell for me to look away from her.

Lorenzo motions with his hand for us to follow him deeper into the palazzo. He seems a raven with the black sleeves hanging off his forearms, wavy white fabric around his wrists.

"If you please." He invites us up the landing to our rooms.

His men follow into Janine's, uninstalling the cameras. But I know Lorenzo too well, and I expect that he'll try to keep at least one, so I check the room myself while he tries to distract Janine, showing her the magnificent view from her window to a lovers' bridge under which gondolas float lazily.

"Oh, look, you missed one." I turn around with the camera I found embedded in the ornate frame of the vanity table mirror.

Lorenzo whips around from the window where he was trying to keep Janine distracted.

"Maybe your men would like to check again, make sure they got them all?"

Hatred crosses Lorenzo's face, which delights me. I will split this asshole's face in two soon, so help me God.

My room is right next to Janine's, and there's even a door between them. Lorenzo locks it and pockets the key.

"Just to make sure you keep a real sense of privacy," he tells Janine. "If your bodyguard wants to visit your chamber he will have to do it by knocking on the front door, on the landing, where there are cameras."

"Fabulous," she replies. "Now, if you don't mind, the conference, the flights, it was all so tiresome. I'd love a bath and a few hours of rest."

"Of course," Lorenzo says. "I do however hope you'll allow me to enjoy your presence at dinner. In about three hours."

"Of course." She gives him a tired smile.

Lorenzo's werewolves show me to the chamber next to Janine's. I take a quick shower, the whole time thinking of ways to break into Janine's room without Lorenzo's surveillance people and devices catching it. I spot and push the surveillance devices in my room just a little bit so that none of them catches the angle to the door between our rooms. I rip a piece of bed spring to pick the lock, but I can't try it yet. Could be that she's still in the bathroom, or walking around that room naked. I close my eyes and channel the power of my six senses to smell and hearing, enhancing them.

She's right there, behind this door, towel-drying her hair. Damn it, she's naked. I breathe in her scent, my cock reacting. It's beyond my control, my body wants her, craves her, needs her. I have to find release, maybe with another woman, and fast, before I do something stupid.

I force myself away from the door so that I can think. Janine's scent is probably the only thing in the world that can make me lose control, and I can't afford that, now less than ever. I sit on the windowsill, making plans of getting to the old secret outposts of my pack in Venice. Even though we haven't been active in Italy for centuries, our people might still be here, leading a quiet life underground, and keeping a low profile. If they're anything like back in the day, they must keep track of the Piovra's moves.

There's a hard knock on the door, and a guy with a thick voice announces dinner. I grab a pair of black denim pants and a black sweater, not caring much about Lorenzo's dress code. The sweater is the loosest item of clothing I brought with me, but I guess I'm too large for anything to ever hang loose on my body, so the sweater is still tight on my arms, shoulders and chest.

The moment Janine and I meet on the landing, my heart stops. *Lady in Red* starts to play in my head. Damn, that song must have been written especially for her. Delicate and feminine in the red dress that hugs the shape of her body in all the right places, she wears it with elegance and style. Her shiny blonde hair that she usually wears in a bob is slicked back, making it look like she's got short hair but, strangely, that only enhances her femininity and grace. It makes her heart-shaped face stand out, black eyeliner contouring her cobalt blue eyes. Damn, it lends those irises even more power of expression, they're cutting right through me.

I look quickly away because I feel all sorts of things I shouldn't feel. I clench my teeth, forcing myself to keep a cool head, but it's so damn hard with her scent of ocean and woman reaching me.

She misinterprets my attitude, of course. She thinks I looked away because I'm not interested, but in truth I'm just hyperaware of her graceful presence beside me as we head to dinner, of the way her delicate muscles move under her white freckled skin. Damn, how I want to kiss those freckles, to put my large rough palms all over her body. I want to be with her, giving her pleasure and taking pleasure from her in return.

"Ah, Janine." Lorenzo stands the moment we enter the dining hall. The fucking idiot feels more attracted to her than he planned, I can tell. Just look at him, eating her alive with those deranged blue eyes.

I hold the chair for her before he gets to, the chair closest to the floor-to-ceiling windows. This dining salon overlooks the romantically lit palazzos across the canal. He's trying to woo her.

"Wow, Lorenzo, this whole scenery seems taken out of a historical romance," Janine says, confirming that she's thinking the same.

"I'm glad you like it."

"Do you dine here every day, or only when you have guests?"

"It's a luxury that I indulge myself in, I must admit," he explains while he spreads the white napkin elegantly on his lap. "As reward for all the responsibility I carry for the entire pack and its business. I'm sure you know from the Wolf brothers what that implies. Or from your own family, you're people who know business and responsibility."

"I've been around the Wolf brothers less than you'd think," she says as the man behind her pours her wine. "And I have been living only in the back offices of my hotels, my travels restricted to conferences and business. I rarely ever stopped to smell the flowers."

"A good thing you're doing it now."

"We're not here to smell the flowers, Lorenzo," I intervene. "We're here because you summoned Janine, interestingly enough on the very day I became her bodyguard."

"A mere coincidence," he says, avoiding my eyes to hide his hatred of me.

"Even if I believed that." I grab a loaf of bread, only to keep my hands busy. I'm not going to eat it. I need meat, the flesh of an enemy freshly torn from his bones. "It still doesn't explain how Janine can help you defeat The Reaper."

"Like I said, some things are better shown than told. But I can tell you this—It has to do with Janine's one night stands."

"Excuse me?" She cocks an eyebrow.

"Your secret escapades with strange men, Janine, that is what drew my attention to you in the first place."

Janine stops breathing.

"Don't worry now, it's not like the entire world knows what you were doing," Lorenzo continues as he starts to cut the meat on his plate. "I wouldn't have found out if I hadn't looked closely at your life either."

He takes his time cutting the roast as we wait for him to continue, his people standing all around the dining salon holding their breath. I can hear Janine's heart beat in her chest, and I smell her body chemistry—she wants to know, but she's not sure she wants it out there, for all these people to hear, especially me.

Part of me doesn't want to know about her sexual encounters with other men either, but the other part wants every detail, it craves to invade her privacy. I hunger to know which one she enjoyed most, if she fell for any of them, if there's anyone she still thinks about when she's doing herself. My fists clench on the table, by the side of my untouched plate.

"After I found out about Darkwood Falls," Lorenzo begins, among bites and taking his sweet time, "I started to dig for more information. Information about the Fated Females of this incredible town. Turned out some of them managed to have a life outside of the town borders despite the serpents' efforts to keep them in. The first escapades we found out about were yours, Janine, and those of Princess Skye, because you are the most prominent women of Darkwood Falls." He angles his head to her. "You're a successful business woman, speaking at conferences and meeting VIPs. But you were too smart to ever hook up with any of them, so you went for random guys in bars, often bikers that you hoped would forget about you as quickly as you forgot about them. Only they didn't."

Bikers. Big, muscular guys that probably pumped her on their Harleys in a way I can only dream of doing. I'm sure Lorenzo enjoys slapping me across the face with all this information, too. Fuck, I can't let him see that it's working.

"What you don't know, Janine," he continues, "What nobody actually knows, is that those hook-ups were not without consequences." He signals to one of his men, who comes forth with a tablet that he places in Lorenzo's outstretched hand. Lorenzo wipes his mouth with the napkin on his lap and turns on the device, revealing the first picture.

It's men. But men that look sicker and sicker with every picture that he swipes over, as if they'd had contact with something radioactive.

"What the hell," Janine whispers as Lorenzo swipes through the pictures.

"All these men have one thing in common, Janine—a one night stand with you, Janine."

"I made them *sick*?" She places a hand on her chest as if to still her heart.

"Well, not exactly," Lorenzo says, pushing the tablet over to me. I swipe through the pictures again, trying to ignore the lump in my throat. Damn it, I don't want to see the men Janine fucked.

"In these pictures they look so sick you expect them to collapse any minute, it's true," Lorenzo goes on. "But even after all these years none of them died. More yet, they underwent multiple tests, and nothing seems to be wrong with them. Well, nothing aside from a slight change in their DNA."

"Change?" Janine whispers.

"All that doctors know is that their DNA has been somehow altered, but they can't tell how that came to affect them, making them look and feel sick even though they aren't. They're still monitoring these guys, in case something changes. And a couple of months ago something did change. May I?"

He holds out his hand for the tablet, but there's no need to hand it over. I've already found it—the picture of a man with a split upper lip, as if his mouth were changing into the snout of a wolf.

"The transformation wasn't complete," Lorenzo fills the silence that has fallen over the salon. Janine is staring with an open mouth at the picture. "Actually, doctors didn't see much behind this except the change in the DNA that must conduce to slight modification of physiognomy, without causing any damage to his biochemistry or his organs, but we are werewolves." I can feel his piercing blue gaze denting my forehead. "We recognize the process behind this picture—this man's body is trying to shapeshift, but the DNA modification wasn't complete. My theory is that he would have shifted completely if he had more nights with you, Janine."

"I'll be damned," she breathes.

Silence fills the salon again, except for the slight shift of fabric when the men move.

Lorenzo laughs. "You should see your face, Conan. You look like a train has just run you over."

"I guess you can say that," I grunt, looking at Janine. "How many were there? How many men did you sleep with?"

Her cobalt blue eyes flash indignantly to mine, as if she can't believe the audacity of my tone. "That's none of your business."

"It turns out you're a Fated Female with a dangerous superpower, Janine. You can turn normal men into werewolves. I've been alive for five centuries and I've never seen anything like this. You're a weapon, and I need to know how many people this weapon has been used on."

"I, I..."

I arch an eyebrow, the scarred one. "What, you don't remember?"

"Hey, don't be a dick," she protests.

"Then don't act like wh—" Janine slaps me.

I'm still trying to understand what just happened when she squares her shoulders, seeming to darken the room. My jaw slackens. I've never seen a woman ooze so much inner strength, especially one as thin and delicate as Janine.

"Listen to me, both of you, because I'm only gonna say this once. I don't owe any of you anything, not even explanations. I've had responsibility weighing on my shoulders since I was a girl, responsibility so heavy I often feared I'd crash, and there was never a man around for me to lean on." She stares straight into my eyes, the hard cobalt in her irises nailing me to my seat. "You, Conan, weren't there when I almost lost everything. You weren't there to lend me a hand or a shoulder when my parents passed, both of them only months apart. When the business they left behind almost went bankrupt, and I desperately searched for a way to salvage what was left of their legacy. You weren't there as I worked myself to exhaustion to numb the loneliness." She points with her finger from me to Lorenzo. "Neither of you was there. I owe either of you *nothing*. You don't get to *demand* answers from me, not in that tone, and sure as hell not with that contemptuous entitlement in your voice."

She pushes back her chair, both Lorenzo and I staring up at her. She looks down at us like a crushing queen, and we can both feel the weight of her personality. I have to grab my cock under the table, make sure it doesn't grow to full length, straining against my fly.

"I'll retire to my chamber now, I need to rest and process all this. I'll think of a way to help these men, because they're living through pain and anguish because of me. But I don't *have* to help you." She juts her chin out at Lorenzo. "You, Lord Piovra, you know what? I don't *have* to help you defeat The Reaper. If anything, I owe my help to the Wolf pack, because they battled Darkwood Falls from the serpents' claws." She glances at me, sharply as a queen. "But that doesn't give you the right to demand answers of me like that, Mr. Wolf. I'm not your girlfriend, your property, or your employee. Mind your tone when you address me again, and when you do, you better start with an apology."

She turns on her heel and leaves the salon, both Lorenzo and I staring after her like puppies.

"Wow," Lorenzo says when she's out of hearing range. "Hot temper."

"Classy temper."

"Well put. She didn't go all bitchy or hysterical even though you almost called her a whore." He grins, and I could fucking slit his throat. "Tell me the truth, Conan, were you jealous? Is that why you talked to her like that?"

I glare at him, both of us locked in a stare-down that expresses all of our bloodlust. "I hope you don't have in mind what I think you do, Lorenzo. Because I'll have your head, then stick it up on a spear right in front of your palazzo."

"A delicious prospect, fighting you again. We'll come to that in due time, but I wouldn't want to spoil it for any of us by starting it too soon."

I push my chair back and stalk down the hall to my chamber.

"Don't leave the palazzo, Conan," Lorenzo calls behind me. "You and Janine are my guests until further notice."

He means prisoners. I defy him by not even looking back, and slamming the door shut behind me. I push the cameras in the bathroom to the side, and rip the mirror off the wall, climbing into the hole and down the piping to the canal under the palazzo. I'm down in the basement and then out into Venice in only a matter of minutes. I slide the hood over my head and slither through the night toward the Wolves' old outpost.

But in a dark corner, under a red light, women with masks and naked breasts pushing out of old-fashioned corsets giggle and beckon clients over. I stop in place. What if?

CHAPTER V

Janine

I'm staring out the window in tears when there's a knock on the door.

"Lord Piovra asking permission to enter," a man with a thick voice announces. I wipe the tears from my face, and gather the silk robe tighter around me. I'll be damned if I let him see the slightest sign of weakness.

"Let him in."

Lorenzo enters the room, his hands clasped together hidden inside the loose black sleeves of his robe, looking like a young priest with a pretty face and the deranged eyes of a serial killer. I lift my chin to show that I'm not scared of him, but I wonder why Conan doesn't make his appearance. He promised he wouldn't ever leave me alone with Lorenzo Piovra.

"I wanted to apologize, Janine," he says. "It was tactless of me, going about things the way I did. I thought maybe you'd like something warm to drink, help you relax and maybe forgive and forget." He makes room for a man to enter carrying in a tray with a vintage tea kettle and two cups on saucers.

"I'll have some tea with you, if you don't mind my company." He smiles, trying to look friendly. "That way you'll be sure I haven't put anything in your drink. Conan surely taught you not to accept anything from me, at least not when he's not there."

I glance to the inside door separating my room from Conan's.

"Wondering why he's not here, I presume," Lorenzo says as he heads to the balcony, where the man sets his tray on the small round table with the wrought iron chairs. "He managed to sneak out of the palazzo, surely to defy me. I reminded him that you were both my guests when he left the dining salon, so I guess he's making a point."

He stands by the balcony table fixing me with a Machiavellian grin. "I guess he didn't foresee that I'd use the chance to speak to you alone, without him intruding all the time. Besides, there are things I think you should know about him. Please, take a seat." He holds a chair for me, everything in his attitude showing I don't have a choice.

With one glance behind me at his men that have flooded my chamber, I take the seat.

"These pretty little Venetian balconies make me think of Romeo and Juliet," Lorenzo says as he pours tea in my cup before he pouring his. Even his voice has become a shade more cutting, hinting at an unstable personality. Makes me think this is a man given to bouts of rage that he glosses over like a psycho. "Have you ever been in love, Janine? Really now, between you and me. Was there ever someone you particularly liked?"

"Years ago, in college. But then..."

"Yes?"

I might as well tell him. "Then I grew up, Lorenzo. I realized that falling in love went hand in hand with low self-esteem. If I fall in love with someone it means that person has traits that I admire, and I feel that I can make those traits mine if I merge with the person. An illusion, a mirage that disappears once you understand it."

I sip. Lorenzo sits frozen with his own cup in his hand, lips slightly parted and eyebrows furrowed as if he's pondering on what I just said.

"Huh," he eventually says. "So you don't believe in love."

"I believe in love in its pure, godly form, if you will. In the love you can feel for any creature, the kind of love that doesn't have to do with sex. To make it clearer, if the feeling is dependent on sexual closeness, then it's one's own complexes and bad self-image working. And hormones."

"Aha. So then you're not in love with Conan Wolf either?"

I burst into laughter, but only because he put his finger right on the wound. "Now why would you think that?"

He shrugs, sipping his tea, looking out at the canal as a gondola passes under the lovers' bridge nearby. I would probably be completely taken with the atmosphere if I weren't so tense about this discussion with this deranged-looking guy, feeling the glares of all his men.

"He's a werewolf, our Conan," he says. "A particularly sexy one, I must admit. Huge, dangerous, the bad-boy every woman would want to tame."

"Women would want to tame him just to prove their own worth. Which is my point exactly."

"So that's why you're so resilient to werewolf charm. Because you know the inner psychological workings of falling in love, and won't fall prey to them?"

"I like to think so, yes."

"That's why I wasn't successful in charming you, either—because, admittedly, I've tried."

"I can't say I haven't noticed."

Lorenzo laughs out loud, the people strolling on the bridge stopping short to place the sound.

"You're a piece of work, Janine. I've never met a woman like you before."

"You have centuries of life experience, and that is the best line you can come up with?"

He snaps at me over the table, making me flinch. Fuck, look at those eyes, his nose furrowing like that of an attacking dog. "You decided you were going to hate me since before you met me, didn't you? And not because of the few books of psycho shit you read, but because Conan created a certain image of me."

"I don't hate you." I clasp my hands on my lap under the table, my shoulders tense. "But I don't trust you either. Please don't take it personally. It's not like I like or trust Conan, either. His brothers Nero and Drago, maybe, but not him."

Lorenzo frowns, interested. I got him. "Why not Conan?"

"Nero and Drago are more, I don't know, humane. Conan is a brute. His feelings are reduced to instinct. His sense of duty towards his family and his people is noble, and I can appreciate that about him, but that's also instinctual."

"So you think that, unlike his brothers, he's more beast than man?"

"I don't know if that's the right way to put it. But he's harder, much more difficult to move."

"That's because Conan has spent over half of his existence in wars, Janine. He's a soldier, a killer. Drago was a gigolo and a cage fighter, Nero a strategist and a businessman, but Conan did the real dirty work. All his life he fought and killed, it's all he's ever known."

"Wow. And I thought you hated his guts. If only he could hear you now, taking his side."

"I hold no love for the man, I'll tell you that, but I do respect him. Still, I think it's a good idea for you to keep emotionally clear of him. It's actually what I've been wanting to talk to you about."

"Oh."

"I'm sorry I exposed you like that in front of Conan, regarding the men in your life."

I look down at my hands. I feel guilty for what happened to those men.

"Is there any way I can help them?"

"If there is, that isn't the reason I invited you here."

I snort. "Finally, you're painfully honest."

"And I'm only just starting." He reaches over the small round table and grabs my arm. I glance from his grip to his face with an outraged look on mine, but it doesn't impress him.

"Janine, Fated Females are special in themselves, but I believe you're even more special than most because you have a superpower—You. Can. Make. Werewolves. I don't know if you realize how huge that is."

For a few moments I just stare at him, wrapping my mind around his point.

"If I had that effect on those men it was because I slept with them, Lorenzo. What are you saying, that you want me to sleep with more, make more of them?"

"I want you to sleep with more, and I want you to do it often, because apparently once isn't enough to finalize the process."

I jump up from the chair, grabbing its wrought iron back, ready to throw it at this monster. "You son of a bitch. You want to make a whore out of me?"

"Calm down, please, I haven't told you everything yet."

"What could you possibly still have to say?"

"Before we even think about making werewolves, I want to imprint on you, Janine."

"What the fuck!" Blood burns my cheeks. "Really, how far can you go?"

"If I imprint on you," he continues, "then all the werewolves that you make will be members of my pack, they would listen to my orders."

"Because, as your mate, *I* would be under your command, right?"

"I suppose you can say that."

"And you think you could share me like that? If what the Wolf brothers told me is true, imprinting on a woman means you fall madly in love with her. You can't even think about another man merely looking at her naked, let alone touch her."

"Yes, but this is the greater good that's at stake. Taking down The Reaper, creating an army so great and so powerful that he won't stand a chance against it."

"Jesus, then how many men do you want me to sleep with?"

"As many as necessary." The coldness in his eyes and in his voice is alarming, the man is deranged. Standing here on this little Venetian balcony, feeling those cold, madman's eyes on me, my skin crawls. I realize the kind of danger I'm in, and how this man could destroy my body and my soul.

"Go to hell," I throw in his face, and turn to the room, pushing his men aside. Surprisingly, they let me pass and stomp to my luggage that's lying open by the wardrobe.

"What are you doing, Janine?" Lorenzo asks half amused as he steps inside after me, moving slowly as if he doesn't have a care in the world. I fear he may have ways in place to keep me here against my will. Actually, what did I expect? Conan warned me, didn't he?

"I'm getting Conan. We're getting out of here."

"I told you, Conan isn't at the palazzo. He's gone out."

"He'll find me, no matter where I am in Venice. He'll catch my scent."

"If you do that, you'd be placing yourself in the hands of a bigger monster than me."

"Maybe. But he would never ask me to become his whore to pass around."

"No, he would probably rip those men's flesh off of their bones and eat it. And it wouldn't even be the first time he'd be doing it."

"What the hell do you mean?"

"You really don't know much about him, do you? He hasn't told you much about himself."

"Just get to the point already." I stand to face him, exasperated. The amusement in his face drives fear into my bones. This man can hurt me with information alone, he doesn't even need to get physical. He's diabolical.

"It's true, what you sensed. Conan is more animalistic than his brothers, more beastly. And that's because of all his war experience. He's a werewolf, strong and resilient, but even werewolves can get PTSD, especially after witnessing so much pain and misery, after losing comrades in battle, seeing them split open right before their eyes and not being able to do anything about it. Centuries ago, Conan was part of a particularly vicious war that led to famine. Stuck in the ruins of a prison town in the cold plains of Russia, Conan and a few others had to survive without food for weeks. In the end, they had no choice but to eat the dead bodies of their comrades, wolves and men. Can you imagine that, Janine? Can you imagine your protector, Conan Wolf, tearing the flesh of his comrades off of their bones with his fangs, a huge brown monster crouched over massacred bodies."

"Stop." I whip around, hiding my face, but Lorenzo continues to advance until I can feel his breath on the side of my face as he brushes my hair behind my ear.

"Do you think a man like that can still have feelings, Janine? To be honest, I don't think there's a human bone left inside him—well, metaphorically speaking."

I remember the intimacy Conan and I shared a few nights ago.

"There was warmth in him," I whisper. "It was there, radiating from his heart to mine, I felt it, even if only for a moment."

"Ah, there it is," Lorenzo whispers satisfied in my ear. "That thing you claimed didn't exist, at least not for you—infatuation."

"I'm not infatuated with him."

"Then why do you insist on seeing the good in him? Why plead for the warmth in his heart?" He pauses, and I realize he must be putting two and two together. "I see. You desire him, and you like to believe he desires you back. Well, I'm sorry I have to disappoint you in this respect as well, Janine."

His arms circle me from behind, bringing the tablet from before between us. My skin crawls at his touch, as I feel his body pressed against my back, but then something worse happens. He shows me a picture that wrenches my heart.

It's Conan, I recognize him by his big muscular back, even though he's wearing a hoodie. He has on the same dark jeans from earlier this evening, tight on his muscular thighs, and the same boots. He's talking to a masked prostitute who's exposing her tits to him under a red light. The next few pictures show frames of the same scene.

"This was taken less than an hour ago."

"Your men followed him?"

"No, but my men are everywhere in Venice. And all of them recognize Conan Wolf when they see him, the carrier of The Reaper's weapon."

"The Reaper's weapon." I lick my parched lips, trying hard to pull myself together. "What is this weapon?"

"I'm afraid I can't tell you that."

"You've already shared so many secrets with me. Why not this one?"

"Because it's a terrible one."

"As terrible as his cannibalizing people?"

"Yes."

He takes distance from me, my back now cold in the breeze of the Venice night.

"Think about my proposition, Janine," Lorenzo says from the door. "Oh, and it might help to know that Conan Wolf has been removed from your service—I instructed my guards not to let him back into the palazzo no matter what."

"What?" I turn around. "Don't you dare, Lorenzo Piovra."

"You have until tomorrow morning to make your decision, Janine—let me imprint on you and help me build an army that will free Darkwood Falls and the entire world from the serpents forever."

"I don't need until tomorrow—it's a freaking *no*!"

"Don't rush. Take into consideration that, in case you refuse, I will have no more use for you than I do for Conan Wolf." He pauses enough for me to understand the death threat. "By the way, if he does make it back to you past the barriers I set up for him, it would be advisable to turn him away. It is very possible that he'll try to imprint on you and therefore render you useless to me. Know that, if this happens, I will kill you on sight. Besides, don't forget he'd be doing it for his own selfish purposes." He waves the tablet at me.

"Mask and tits under a red light. What was that you said about the warmth you felt from him?"

With that he exits my room, his men trailing after him. The door falls shut and I stare at it for moments. When I finally grasp what just happened, everything playing like a rapid movie before my eyes, I collapse on the floor, crying hard. Many people have tried to break me in my life, but I'm afraid Lorenzo Piovra might just succeed.

Janine

MY EYES HURT AS I STARE out into the dawn. I haven't looked into the mirror, because what's the point, but I know I must look like shit. I'm wearing the same night robe as yesterday, and I don't plan on changing. I can already hear the echo of Lorenzo's men up the stairs, and I know he's coming for my decision.

I've spent the night imagining all the ways his proposition would destroy me. I've met forced prostitutes in my life, and many came to feel so worthless they became suicidal. I'm sure it wouldn't be any different for me.

Lorenzo appears in the doorway. I can only see his shape from the corner of my eye, my mouth distorting as I swallow my disgust. He waits there for a few moments, expecting my decision. I finally turn, glaring at him with all the hatred I'm capable of, but I don't say anything.

"So it's a no after all," he says, feigning disappointment. He steps inside the room, hands behind his back like a pondering wise man. "You know what's funny, Janine, that you actually thought you had a choice."

"Don't I?" I cried so much my voice sounds like a crow's. Lorenzo faces me with those pale blue eyes, a slight smile on his face that doesn't do anything to hide his readiness to hurt me if he has to.

"I need you Janine," he says. "I won't be able to do this without you, so I can't really afford to offer you a choice."

"I'd rather die than sleep with a whole army of men."

"Come on, would it really be so different from what you were doing in secret on your nights outside of Darkwood Falls?"

I fill my stare with all the contempt I feel for him. "I slept with a few guys over the course of ten years, and you think that means I could sleep with just anybody?"

"Come on, Janine, you make it sound a lot worse than it is. First of all, after the imprinting ceremony you'll be loved beyond your wildest dreams. I will give you my heart, I'll love you completely and madly. Building the army is going to be as devastating to me as it will be to you."

"You don't have a heart to give, you son of a bitch."

"Tsk, tsk, tsk, please, my mother doesn't have anything to do with this." He approaches me, lifting my chin up so that we look into each other's eyes. "This means more to me than you know, and I'll prove it. I'll make our first experience together special."

I spit in his face, right here in front of his men. "If this is gonna cost me my soul," I say under my breath, "then I'll make sure it costs you your image, you narcissistic bastard."

Lorenzo's pretty boy features harden, showing his anger, and I half expect him to slap me. But he just turns his back to me, commanding his people something in Italian.

A couple of women enter the room, both from the fashion industry from the look of them. I struggle, determined to resist and not let them make me look appealing to that monster Lorenzo, but one of his men slings me over his shoulder, carrying me to the bathroom and dropping me into the bathtub. My screams and struggles are met with blank faces and a hard grip on my jaw and hands. By the time I exit the room in a long white silk dress, and smelling like a rose as if it were my wedding day, I have bruises around my wrists and on my neck. I guess it's not gonna bother Lorenzo, though.

He's crazy if he thinks I'll give in without a fight. As they escort me down to the canal underneath the palazzo and to the gondola I make plans in my head, picturing all the ways I can make Lorenzo's life a living hell after he imprints on me. It's only a little while after my gondola has taken a turn and drifted onto a dark canal that I realize that something's wrong.

I turn around, looking up at the gondolier, a female with olive complexion. Italian, I would say. She's young, not wearing any make-up, but a hood over her head, her dark eyes fixed on a point in front of her.

A chill enwraps me as I look around at the decaying palazzos. We must be in a less frequented part of Venice. The waters seem colder, and the walls retain more chill, because they're unrenovated, and in ruin. I recognize the corner with the red light, but when I turn to ask the woman for an explanation it's no longer her that I see. It's Conan. The gondola has reached a set of stone stairs, and he's reaching out to help me.

"Come on," he whispers, and I take his hand, forgetting all my grievances with him and happy beyond belief that he saved me from Lorenzo.

The first thing he does when I'm up on the dock is touch a finger to my lips, hushing me before I can open my mouth to speak, placing the other hand on the small of my back. I let him guide me inside what seems to be a bustling renaissance pub, or more like a brothel. Half-naked men and women with masks on their faces and drinks in their hands mingle with each other, their laughter mixing with the music.

Conan guides me to a small room at the very back of the establishment, a room that hookers must use with their clients, judging by the bed with silks and velvets, cushions, and side table with oils and perfumes. He closes the door and turns around, pushing the hood off his head.

Relief drains the blood from my head and I collapse to the floor, covering my face with my palms and sobbing hard. The floorboards shake under Conan's steps as he walks to me, clasping my shoulders and pulling me up into his arms.

"What the hell, Conan." I beat his chest. "Why the fuck did you leave me alone at Lorenzo's palazzo, why did you leave me behind in that monster's claws?"

"I can explain." His deep voice vibrates against my hands as I unclasp my fists and splay my fingers over his boulder-hard pectorals, greedy for the reassurance that he is really here.

"You." I sniffle. "You left me in order to go and fuck a hooker. But Lorenzo took the chance and came to my room, said things, did things."

He clasps my arms, bringing me up on my toes, forcing me to look into his reddish eyes. The scar running down his face makes him look like a killer who's just spotted his target. "*Did* things? What did he do to you?"

Crying like crazy I tell him all about last night with Lorenzo, the things he said and what he planned to do with me. When I'm finished I'm sitting on the bed, wretched and sniffling, Conan standing in front of me, looking like he could tear Lorenzo's head off his shoulders.

"And you couldn't protect me," I cry out. "You weren't there. You were here, with a hooker, and his men saw you and took pictures."

He roars and punches the wall, making me flinch and lift my knees up to protect myself. My mouth pops open as I look at the hole he just left in the wall. Jesus Christ, his fist actually broke through the bricks into the next room.

"Jesus," I whisper.

Conan kneels in front of me, grabbing my waist and pulling me close. God, his fist is bloody.

"Lorenzo just tried to come between us. It was not what it looked like with that woman. But that bastard will stop at nothing to imprint on you, Janine. He'll hunt you down your entire life if he has to, you won't be safe from him till the day you die."

"And what do you suggest that I do? Because, I'd rather die than ever be with that bastard."

He presses his eyes shut as if the idea hurts him. "Don't say that, please. For as long as he stalks you I will be shadowing you, shielding you from him. But that will have to come at a price."

I give him a bitter smile. "Of course. Letting you imprint on me, isn't it, that's the price? He said you might try something like this."

"You don't understand."

"Oh, I think I do. Now that you know what I'm worth, you're reconsidering your decision of never imprinting. All for your own selfish reasons, just as Lorenzo predicted."

"Janine, I don't have to imprint on you. But I will have to protect you from him at all times, meaning that this time you'll have absolutely no privacy left. I'll never let what happened yesterday happen again."

"It wouldn't have happened yesterday either if you'd been there," I snap at him, ready to cry and put more blame on him, but he cups my face with his big rough palm, looking deeply into my eyes as if he can feel my pain.

"I had to leave, and I had to do what I've done. It was part of the plan."

"Argh," I cry out in frustration, trying to slap his hand from my face but it doesn't move him at all. "Part of the plan, seeing a hooker under a red light? You can't fool me, Conan, because I saw the pictures. I saw you standing close to her, your chest touching her naked tits." I bring my face to his, the heat of rage radiating off my skin. "You say you'll be my bodyguard forever? I'm afraid I have to disappoint you on that one, because I made a different decision. As soon as I meet another werewolf, one who isn't Lorenzo Piovra, one of his men, or one of your brothers, I'm gonna let him imprint on me. I'll give myself to someone else, Conan, so neither you nor Piovra will win this war."

Conan's hand hardens, his rough palm scraping my cheek as it slides to the back of my head, sinking into my hair and grabbing a fistful.

"And how long do you think your new werewolf lover would survive after he's tasted you?"

"If you killed him, I'd die too, wouldn't I? Imprinting makes the female love so binding that she'd die for her mate, Arianna and Princess told me that."

"Oh, but I wouldn't let you die, you see. I'd tie you up in a cottage deep in the woods where no one would find us. Where no one could ever take you away from me."

He tugs my hair just a little, but I can feel all the strength that he's holding back. The hole in the wall stands witness to just how much damage the hand fisted in my hair can do. But then Conan takes over my mouth, and I stop thinking.

He lays me back on the bed, his hand cupping my head as he pushes his tongue into my mouth, forcing my lips apart. Oh, God, is he trying to imprint on me against my will?

I struggle under him and he lifts his body off me, looking me in the eyes. He's between my legs, his rock hard manhood pushing against my folds through his jeans and the flowing fabric of my almost-wedding-dress.

"Conan, look at me. If you make me yours, it will be against my will."

He pushes his cock harder against me, my legs parting more, my knees emerging from under the folds of my gown.

"I wouldn't dream of taking you against your will," he breathes. "I will make you beg for it."

He claims my mouth in a deep kiss, his fingers splaying in my hair.

"Your hair is so silky," he says gruffly.

"Conan, stop." I try not to pant, but as he goes down, kissing my neck, then trailing down my chest, my judgement clouds. He parts the sides of my dress with his fingers, then cups my breasts with those big rough palms that could crush rocks.

"Ah," he breathes, his eyes closed as he takes in the sensation of my flesh filling the palms of his hands.

"Don't you touch me like that after you had your hands on that hooker," I protest, pushing him away and starting to kick my legs. He grabs my wrists, doing nothing but accepting my rage, but his now blood-red irises betray the dangerous thoughts in his head.

"If you think that I betrayed you," he says, "punish me." He pulls my wrists to the side, my naked chest bumping into his abs, rock-hard under the black hoodie.

"Use me," he says in a gruff voice that works like a drug in my head. He goes down, still keeping his grip on my wrists, and buries his head between my legs.

All I can see is the dark hood over his head as his muscular shoulders slip under my thighs and his hard mouth touches me between my legs. The sensation courses through me and I moan, trying to pull away, but he pushes his face harder into my pussy.

There's nowhere I can go, now at the mercy of his lips and his tongue as his hands keep me pinned down to the bed. He slides his tongue between my folds, right over my clit. My thighs clench, which tells him he's just hit the sweet spot. I groan, expecting him to go down on me viciously, forcing the pleasure on me, but then surprise.

He goes slowly, teasing, making me push myself to his mouth and plead for more with my whole body.

"Do you want me to stop now?" he says against my creamed folds.

"You know I don't."

He kisses my pussy passionately, as if fueled by my words, and I arch from my waist, giving myself to him. "Ah, please let me cum, and get it over with."

"Janine." He moves up my body until his face is right above mine. God, he drives me crazy with his looks, a mercenary with a scarred face and blood-red eyes. Determined to make me his. He pins my wrists beside my head as his need-filled gaze pierces me. "Back in Nice you promised me something. You offered to do whatever I asked of you when we came here, to Venice, remember that?"

"What are you getting at?"

"The time has come for you to deliver on that bargain. And this is what I'll have of you—use me for your pleasure. Take from me what you want, make me your slave. But make me your slave forever."

"What the hell are you saying?" I breathe, searching his eyes, the eyes of a madman.

"I won't be your bonded mate, if you don't want that. But through our union, I'll become your bonded servant. In all ways. Think about it. I'll do your every bidding, I'll even kill for you."

"I would never command you to kill anyone—"

"No? Not even Lorenzo, for what he did to you?"

I can't deny I'd love to see Conan's huge fist shattering Lorenzo's psycho face.

"That would still mean that you imprint on me."

His knuckles go white as his grip tightens on my wrists. "You don't understand, Janine. You will never be with another man anyway. You either accept *me*, or you'll remain single forever, because I'll kill any man who ever gets close to you."

I open my mouth to say something, but I can't, not when he's got this look on his face. He will follow through with his promise, I can see it.

"I don't know what you've done to me, Janine," he whispers. He bends down to my cheek and kisses me right under my ear, the soft touch sending delicious prickles all over my skin. "I didn't imprint on you in France, and yet my feelings are spinning out of control." He keeps kissing my jaw and neck gently as he talks, but I can feel that he's holding back ardent desire to do more. "I could stare at you for hours, days, weeks, a lifetime without getting tired of it."

"You don't mean that. Nobody ever means that." I whisper.

"My brothers feel that way about your friends. They are the living proof, wouldn't you say?" He face hovers over mine. God, how can I resist him when he looks at me like that?

"I will take you, Janine." His breath touches my face as he begins grinding his big hard cock against my folds. He brings my wrists together above my head, pinning them in one hand, while the other lifts my gown, searching for my nakedness.

"Ah, you're so smooth." His fingers stroke over my naked creamed flesh, his moves harder, more urgent. "And all mine."

I pant as he pumps me without entering me, my most private parts exposed to him while his jeans are still on. It makes me feel so vulnerable, at the whims of a beast.

"I'll have you deliver on our bargain from Nice now, Janine. You'll let me enter you, and use me for your pleasure."

I don't find it in myself to protest when he frees his erection. I look down at the engorged purple head of his manhood before he pushes it inside of me, causing me to arch my back and my mouth to open.

Ache and pleasure mix, butterflies exploding in my stomach. Conan Wolf's big hard cock slides between my slick walls, filling me. Someone pinch me, because I can't believe this is actually happening, at least not until the door flies open and a giggling couple stumbles in.

My head snaps to the side towards them, but I still can't emerge from the euphoric state I'm in. Conan pumps me harder and harder as if nothing happened, as if he doesn't even perceive them. The woman's tits hang out of her cleavage like the woman's I saw in the picture with Conan, and the man is wearing a mask that covers only his eyes, so the expression of their faces is fully exposed to me.

Those pictures Lorenzo showed me of Conan and the hooker return in flashes, ravaging my heart. I struggle under Conan, but his clasp on my wrists only becomes firmer as he fucks me harder. He doesn't mind the intruders who can't seem to take their eyes off of us.

I stop struggling under him, taking in the ache and pleasure of his huge cock inside of me, staring fascinated at his transformation. It doesn't take a genius to realize he's shifting into a werewolf as he fucks me, and my want for him picks up like a whirlwind. His muscles burst out through his hoodie, shattering the fabric as dark brown fur sprouts out all over him, his face morphing into that of a devil from renaissance paintings, not really like an animal, and yet so much like a beast.

I'm being taken like a princess bride by a huge, muscular beast that's driving his cock deep inside me, which feels so dirty and yet heavenly. I can't fight the build-up of pleasure inside of my body, I rejoice in feeling his claws on my wrists, his bright eyes on me, his beastly lips curling over metallic fangs as he spills his seed inside of me. His huge cock pulses against my slick walls as he cums, groaning through his dangerous fangs.

I twist my hands to grab his claws, not caring that I cut myself on them, and cum hard around him, giving him my essence, surrendering myself to him like an offering on an altar. And he enjoys it, he takes it in with greedy eyes as he gives me pleasure that shakes my entire body.

By the time he falls exhausted on the bed to my side, morphing back into a human, a naked one with glistening muscles from the exertion and the pleasure, I've forgotten about the intruders. Until the man whispers, "What the fuck."

I sit up, startled, just in time to see the woman turn to the man, take his masked head between her hands and say, "Sight be blind, never cast behind, this moment fades into the twilight veils."

The man's limbs turn mellow and he falls to the ground. The woman's eyes meet mine. My mind is ravished after the wild lovemaking with a werewolf, but still clear enough to understand she's a witch. One who knows about werewolves, and who's just hexed her client into forgetting all about it.

CHAPTER VI

Conan

"What in the world is she doing?" Janine inquires as I drive the gondola down the dark Venice canals in the night. She's staring at Cinzia, the 'intruder witch', as she's spraying the air with one of her self-brewed perfumes.

"The scent will mask your natural smell," the woman explains. "Because otherwise the werewolves would track you both by your scent."

Janine clutches the black wool cape around herself, her breath misting the air. Her natural scent reaches me, and I have to fight myself not to react. The need to look at her all the time pools in the pit of my stomach, and her scent only makes it worse.

I feel her gaze moving slowly from me to Cinzia and back again as the gondola glides along the narrow canals, sending ripples toward the old walls. I can feel she's still struggling to wrap her mind around things, but I told her it was better to keep quiet until we got to the sanctuary, where she would get answers. Piovra's werewolves could pick up the sound of our voices, and track us down.

With focus and stealthy methods we reach the sanctuary safely, namely the old prison under the Doge's palace.

"You gotta be kidding me," Janine whispers as we enter what used to be the chief prison ward's office back in the day.

"You want me to send for them now?" Cinzia inquires.

"No, wait until further notice from me."

"But my lord—"

"Do as I tell you."

With a final glance from Janine to me she closes the door, and I pull the heavy iron latch after her.

"So," Janine's voice is small and shaky. "This is the famous sanctuary. Are you going to take me again, without waiting for my consent?"

I turn to her, allowing my eyes to roam all over her the way I've been craving to do since we stepped into the gondola. She looks confused and ravished. I tower over her as she stares up at me.

It's no secret that I imprinted on her. She's now my mate, she belongs to me. She saw me in my wolf form, and came for me in that shape, which means she accepted my imprinting fully. That's a very special thing to happen, most mated couples don't get that for a while.

"You hungered for me as much as I did for you," I drawl. I know her legs are trembling under the wool cape, and not because of the chill but because of our wild love-making. They give in, and she takes a seat on the cot by the far wall, exhausted.

"Arousal is not consent, Conan," she manages, her voice shaky. She looks away from me, to the shelves of books along the walls, books that haven't been touched in many years.

"You didn't protest either, because you knew I would have stopped. I wouldn't have taken you against your will, no matter what."

"You used our bargain from Nice against me."

"And then you took me happily between your thighs."

She stares up at me, her blonde hair and her pale face shimmering in the moonlight.

"Janine." I hunker down in front of her, placing my hands gently on her knees. "I need you to understand something. I didn't imprint on you in order to prove a point. I did it because I felt irresistibly drawn to you, like a moth to a flame, and because I couldn't bear the thought of you ever belonging to someone else. I would have killed anyone you would have fallen for, out of jealousy and unhealthy infatuation. I didn't need to imprint on you in order to feel that.

"It's true that I only made the decision to take you *after* you said that you didn't want Piovra, that you hated him. But I don't think he would have really forced you to prostitute yourself for him. The idea alone would have destroyed his soul. Imprinting gives us werewolves feelings that..." I wet my lips, searching for a way to explain. "They're overwhelming."

Pain furrows the white, almost translucent skin on her forehead. She looks down at my hands on her knees. "He knows what imprinting would feel like," she whispers. "And he doesn't care."

"Please, Janine, believe me when I tell you he doesn't have a clue. I knew more or less what to expect because I have a link to my two brothers who experienced it already. Lorenzo can't possibly imagine, because none of the werewolves in his pack have ever imprinted. But trust me, he would have felt as protective of you as I do. And most probably as possessive, as mad, as jealous."

Her cobalt blue eyes fill with a mysterious feeling. "I can't forget the pictures of you and that woman under the red light. Her naked breasts were brushing against your body while I was alone at Lorenzo's palazzo, completely at his mercy."

"I can explain."

"Then you better start talking."

I kind of like the tone of her voice. "Are you jealous?"

"It's not a good thing, Conan, and it's not doing me any favors. My rational mind understands that these women know about werewolves, that they're witches and they must be some kind of allies, but—"

"They are allies that have been here for hundreds of years, laying low so that the Piovras wouldn't track them down. Their connection to the Wolf pack is secret, and it must stay that way, which is why they use prostitution as their cover." I take Janine's small cold hands between mine. "Which brings us to the reason why I brought you here, to the old prison under the Doge's palace. This, Janine, is the Wolf pack's old Venice headquarters."

I get up to my feet and head to the shelves, picking a book so old that the pages stick together, caked by humidity. I separate the pages with careful fingers, walking back to Janine.

"Two centuries ago the Wolf pack and the Piovras became allies. It was Nero's decision, but I had doubts. I didn't trust Lorenzo and his pack. But we had to work together, fight together against the serpents. On the one hand we needed them, but on the other hand we knew they were dangerous, and we had to watch our backs. Especially as Lorenzo, being a power-monger, wanted nothing more than to get his hands on The Reaper's secret weapon. He'd been searching for it for a long time."

I lose myself in memory, my eyes stuck to the sacred geometry spreading over the pages.

"What is this famous secret weapon, Conan? And why is it so important to Lorenzo?"

"Because it's immensely powerful."

"Why don't you just tell me what it is? I am your bonded mate, I can never betray you."

"I can't tell you or anyone because its power can corrupt. Even the most pious, pure and selfless can come to desire it for themselves. But the problem with the weapon is that it can destroy its holder. It takes a powerful carrier to wield it." I shake my head. "Please, don't ask any more questions about this."

Janine comes to my side and looks down into the book at the beautiful, symmetrical drawings. Her eyes brighten, and her intelligent face comes to light.

"Is this Sacred Geometry?" She moves her hand over the book, but doesn't touch the paper. Her fingers tremble as they hover above the pages, as if she respects them too much to touch them.

I take her hand and guide it to the old page, tracing the raven eye on the heading. "The Witch Eyed Sisters. The order to which the women from the brothel belong."

"An order of witches. Why in the world do they work as hookers?"

"How else would they keep track of everything that happens in this town, from the mafia to politicians?"

"Of course," she whispers. "The best-informed people everywhere in the world—hookers, drug dealers, the homeless guy on the busiest street. But does that mean you didn't sleep with that woman?"

I place my hands on her shoulders, pulling her close. "I admit that was my intention when I first left the palazzo, but only because I couldn't stop thinking about you, wanting you like a madman. I became possessive of you, I felt things I didn't understand, and I wanted to lose those feelings because they hurt. But then I saw Cinzia and my focus shifted. I recognized the Witch Eyed Sister."

Janine presses her lips together, forming a thin line. "So your feelings for me weren't strong enough to keep you interested only in me."

"On the contrary. That was exactly the reason I *needed* to find release with another woman. But I don't think I could have gone through with it. I would have seen your face all the while."

I caress her cheek, my eyes roaming hungrily all over her face. She closes her eyes as my lips touch hers, at first gently, but then I lose control. I pull her in my arms, pressing her delicate body to my battle-hardened chest.

"Ah, Janine, I want you so much I don't know how to handle it."

"I guess we're both new to this," she whispers, her breath hot on my lips as we kiss.

We undress each other, our bodies full of fire. I lay her down on the cot, my rough hands sliding appreciatively over her naked body as her eager hands move down my hips.

I claim her mouth with hot, needy lips, as she grabs my cock in her small white hand. I wince at the slight discomfort. It's a greedy, clumsy grab, but it's her, and therefore it feels like heaven. I raise myself on my arms, my muscles turning to ropes under my skin. She strokes my triceps with her fingertips, hissing as if it delights her. The pleasure she gives me stroking my cock up and down, fully naked and sweaty with desire under me, while I still have my pants on, makes me want her like a beast.

"I never thought I could want a woman like this, Janine." I breathe hard, barely still controlling myself. There's that prickle under my skin, like a thousand marching ants as my muscles grow and the fur starts sprouting.

"That's it, shift for me, lover." Her gaze is fluid with desire, as if having me inside her in my wolf form is her favorite brand of kink, her hand wrapped tightly around my big ribbed cock.

"Janine," I breathe, claiming her mouth in a possessive kiss, positioning myself between her legs and entering her in one long, slow push.

"Oh, God, Conan," she cries, arching her back as I fill her, her fingernails scratching my shoulders, and I love it.

I pump into her slowly, the fur sinking back into my skin.

"I won't take you as a wolf tonight," I tell her, watching her face as I fuck her, freely, not caring about the consequences. "I want to feel your touch on me, your fingernails scratching my skin. Do it harder."

She hesitates.

"Do it Janine." I cup the crown of her head with my huge palm, pushing my chest into hers. "Claw at me until you draw blood."

She tries, but my skin is too thick. I consciously lessen the density, allowing her to pierce me. She hisses with pleasure.

"Tell me the truth, my sweet lover—do you enjoy hurting me?"

Her face is red with the exertion, her chocolate eyebrows furrowed as she takes in the pleasure and ache from my thrusts, but she bites her lip to keep the answer in, probably wanting to deny her dark desire.

"Don't even try. We're bonded mates now, we cannot lie to each other. Whenever I, your bonded lover, will ask you a question, you'll be compelled to answer me with the truth. And I will respond with the same honesty."

"I want to punish you, Conan," she pants. "Because you ignored me in the beginning. Because you didn't fall in love with me at first sight."

That's not true, I felt compelled to stare at her from the beginning, but that's beside the point. My head swims with hot desire, and I want her to hurt me nonetheless. "Give me your punishment, woman."

Her nails pierce deeper, biting past my skin into my flesh. I cum hard inside of her as little streams of hot blood trickle down my back, Janine splaying her hands over my shoulder blades, smearing the blood over them. Moments later, as I lie face down on the cot with my hands under my chin and she lies on my back, caressing my shoulders, she says,

"They look like wings of an angel."

"I'm afraid I'm no angel, Janine. Perhaps a fallen one, in the best case scenario," I whisper with my eyes half closed, high on our love making, and enjoying the fulfillment inside. It's an exquisite feeling that I wish would last forever.

I turn on my back and pull her to my chest, cupping her small delicate jaw with my hand.

"I'd stay here with you forever," she whispers sweetly, drawing gentle circles on my chest with her fingertips. "I'd spend my entire life in your arms. But I don't know about the neck pain." She taps my chest. "Your body feels like a rock."

I smile, closing my eyes as I enjoy the warmth of her body on mine, her voice and her scent of ocean and woman. "If only I could do something about it."

"I mean it, Conan." She touches my chin, making me look down at her. Every time I do she's more beautiful, and I swear my soul is melting into hers.

"I want to spend every second of my life with you, even if that means staying here, in this prison cell forever."

"It's not a cell, it's the old office of the chief prison ward."

"It doesn't make any difference." Her cobalt blue eyes melt into loving velvet, her voice caressing me. "I say it with all my heart, I wouldn't mind if it were years, if it's forever. Even though I must admit these feelings inside scare me. They're so intense they can't possibly be healthy. Normal people need their little freedoms, and I more than anyone. I didn't even think myself capable of falling in love, and yet look at me, completely at the mercy of your attention."

I smile lovingly. "I suppose we're both hard people who've become each other's soft spot." But then a particular thought sends a blade through my heart. My body turns rigid, and Janine notices.

"What is it?"

"Nothing."

"You try to smile, but your cheek twitches." She sits up, her palms splayed on my pectorals. The sight of her sitting up like a naked queen looking down at me sends a rush to my cock. I'm ready to take her again, but her face is much too serious for me to try. "You can't lie to me you say, now that our mates' bond is fully forged. Very well then. What made you tighten up like that? What crossed your mind?"

My jaw sets, but Janine stares demandingly into my face, waiting for an answer.

"I was thinking about your one night stands. I was wondering how many men there were in your life." My heart cringes as I expect her to lash out at me.

Janine lifts her chin, looking like a nymph made of ivory in the moonlight, the shadows of the barred window above our heads falling on her face that has become guarded.

"Five," she says. "It was five one night stands. Before that I had two more-or-less long-time boyfriends, both from Darkwood Falls. But I never really expected much from those relationships."

"Fuck," I grunt. "I thought it would do me good to know, but it feels like shit."

"Then why don't you drop the subject?"

"Because I can't."

"Well, then I hope you're in for one hell of a fight."

"All right." I sit up on my elbows, staring into her addictively beautiful face. Deep down I know that the more I'll look at this face, the more I'll want to see it, but now the ball is rolling, and there's no turning back. "Then answer me this—have you ever been in love before?"

"I have. But not as intensely as I am with you."

"That's normal, because no human bond can compare to imprinting, but still." I take her face in my hands, letting them slide through her silky hair to the back of her head. "The way I feel about you is out of this world, Janine, ripped from the hottest depths of hell. I need to know if you feel the same about me, or I'm gonna go insane."

"Conan, I just told you I'd spend every second of my life with you, and I meant that literally, isn't that declaration of love enough?"

"It does feel like a shot of adrenaline, but I can't help the jealousy. Thinking that you've had other men, enjoyed their touch, the feel of their cocks inside you, I—" I bite my lip, drawing blood. I expect Janine to fight back with a counter-argument but what she does is press her lips to mine, her tongue licking the blood off of my lip.

"I'm sorry, I couldn't resist," she says, staring at me as if she doesn't quite understand what's happening. But I do.

"Our bond deepens by the second," I explain. "It urges us to become one with each other. Your instincts scream to take the fluids of my body inside your own, and for me to take yours."

Janine crushes her lips to mine, her arms winding around my neck as if she's abandoning herself to this love that takes us both in a whirlwind. We fall together back on the cot and I plunge into her, roaring and grinding until the iron frame gives in under us.

Janine

CONAN'S ARMS WIND AROUND me, keeping me close and warm on the lovers' bridge.

"Isn't this dangerous," I whisper, my breath turning to mist in the night.

"It is," he whispers back. "But I wanted you to enjoy Venice, at least a little bit. And especially the full moon."

I turn in his arms and look up at his hard warrior face, tracing the scar running down his cheek. If once it made him look dangerous, now it speaks to me of pain. I want to talk to him about it, but we have to keep verbal communication to a minimum. We've got Cinzia's special perfume to mask our scent from Lorenzo's hounds, but they can track our voices, too.

Conan's big hand puts slight pressure on my hip, the signal that we better return to our hideout. We've been here in Venice for a few weeks already, making love in the old prison as if not doing it would starve us, Conan telling me about the werewolf lore and history as I lay in his arms on the mattress. But we're still not even close to getting enough of each other. In fact, if anything, we want each other more with every hour we spend together.

"Does it ever get warm and comfortable," I say as I take off the wool cape back at the sanctuary, before we even enter the old prison ward's office. "This need we have for each other?" I reach up as he lifts me in his arms. I wind my legs around his waist, kissing him hungrily as he walks into the room and pushes the door shut, but something's off about the place.

We find Cinzia in a black cape in the place where we should see an old wooden bookcase. She has a hood over her head, and a dark tunnel stretches out behind her. I realize it must be a secret exit from the sanctuary.

"Apologies for intruding, my lord," she says. Her eyes move from Conan to me under her hood. "But you need to leave. Now. The Piovras are raiding the entire city for you. They could discover the hidden tunnels. If you're planning on using them, now's the time."

This isn't a surprise to either of us. Conan and I have been talking about this, and we're ready. Conan lights the torch, sprays oil over the bookshelves, and looks at them one last time before he sets them on fire. The Piovras can never get their hands on the Wolves' secrets and, while we take along the most important scrolls and manuscripts, the rest needs to be either protected or destroyed.

The fire roars behind us as Conan rushes with me down the narrow dark corridors that smell dank and old, Cinzia trailing behind us. We slide into a gondola that Cinzia's got ready deep down, and Conan pushes us off the dock.

But as we glide silently on the water ripples with only the sound of our hearts pounding in our ears, I get a strange feeling. Something about Cinzia just isn't right. The way her eyes dart around as she sits in the gondola in front of me, both of us bracing ourselves under our capes against the chill and the mist, it's suspicious. She searches the area not as if she were looking for threats, but like she's waiting for them.

Then I spot something in the night as it flies at Conan.

"Watch out!" I cry out, pointing at it. But it's too late.

A large wolf materializes from the darkness like a spreading net, falling on Conan's back. He doesn't manage to throw the large Conan overboard, but the impact sends the gondola rocking on the canal like on a raging sea. Both Cinzia and I fall to the side, grabbing the edges of the gondola and staring up at the struggling men.

Conan roars and throws the attacker off of him, water splashing onto the gondola as the wolf sinks like a bomb into the canal. Conan reaches out to help us up, but two more werewolves attack him. They fail to throw him down, but the gondola sways dangerously, both Cinzia and I screaming. I'm flat on my stomach, holding tightly to the edge of the gondola, a veil of water hanging on my lashes, but I can still see Conan. He balances the gondola with his muscular legs while tearing the wolves off of him, but more of them jump from the darkness, overwhelming him. They bury him in a heap of fur, their deadly roars tearing through the night.

The gondola tips over, and a vacuum pulls at my ears, water invading my nostrils. Then it all goes black.

Conan

I FURROW MY BROW, STRUGGLING to clear the fog in my head. What the hell happened? I look up to the only source of light in this chilly darkness, a pain in the back of my neck. It's just an opening above my head, sending a cone of light down to where I'm standing, naked and in chains.

Something sharp slides across my wrists like blades. Heavy iron cuffs are restraining my arms to the side, and I'm clearly in a dungeon. My muscles hurt with every move, maybe because of the weight I've had on me—all those wolves with their battle-hardened bodies.

"Why did you have to fall for her, my lord," Cinzia's voice with its thick accent reaches me from the darkness.

"Witch Eyed Sister." I sound hoarse, as if my vocal cords were rusty. "What did you do?"

"Why, I betrayed you, of course." She steps into the light, wearing a fresh cape, a dark-red one. She pushes the hood off her head, revealing rich dark hair and shimmering dark eyes.

"But please don't think it was my intention from the start, because it wasn't. It is true, however, that when Lorenzo stormed the establishment with his people I didn't take a lot of convincing to tell him where you were. It was your life or mine. And why should I give up breath for you?"

She steps closer, letting me see the fury and frustration in her face.

"You and I can never be," I say. "And you know why."

"Long ago you said you didn't want to imprint on any woman, ever, and that you wouldn't do it even if you met a Fated Female."

"And you took that as a personal promise I made to you?"

"Maybe I did. I was even prepared to be with you without asking for your love. I was determined to love enough for the both of us. All because you said the more people a werewolf loved, the weaker he was. And I took you seriously, even when you said that the love for a Fated Female could be deadly." She snorts. "Look at you now. I guess you were right."

She paces around me, inspecting my battered, bloody body from all angles. "Do you know what it felt like to find you fucking her with so much gusto in *my* whoring room? Do you have any idea how much I dreamt about you fucking *me* like that, in your wolf form?"

"Cinzia..."

"Why, my lord? Why didn't you ever do it? Damn it, I would have done the dirtiest things with you, I would have been your whore."

"What happened with Janine, it was beyond my control. What she and I feel for each other, it was never up to us."

"Lies!" She cries. "You lied on that first night you came to me, saying you needed to rescue her for wholly other reasons than your feelings. You said you wouldn't imprint on her for the world."

"And I meant it." I glare at her out of red-hot eyes. "I couldn't let Lorenzo imprint on her, it would have been a disaster. Janine has a superpower, Cinzia, and Lorenzo could take over the entire world using it, fuck, rescuing her probably stopped the apocalypse."

"Damn it, even the way you pronounce her name betrays your passion for the woman!"

"Passion, yes." My arms strain against the chains, clattering them powerfully from the walls. Cinzia takes a step back. "Passion beyond rhyme or reason, and beyond my control. Since the day I met Janine feelings started to bubble up inside of me, and there was nothing I could do to stop them. I didn't understand those feelings at first, because I'd never experienced them before, but after Nice they became unbearable. I couldn't look at her without wanting her, and God knows I tried to. It's the reason I was looking for a hooker that night. I was desperate for release, for a way to stop obsessing about Janine Kovesi. But then I ran into you, and a plan started to take shape in my head."

Cinzia's lips draw in a straight, angry line. "In my mind, we had a deal the two of us—I would accept your lack of love for me, as long as you didn't give that love to someone else. But then you went ahead and fucked Janine Kovesi, giving her your heart in the process."

"I did," I hiss. "And you know what? I'd let myself be tortured just to have her one more time."

She stares at me full of revenge. "Be careful what you wish for, my lord."

⊙⊗

Conan

"TORTURE," LORENZO SAYS, staring at me out of pale blue eyes. "You would take torture just to be with Janine one last time?"

"I'd let you skin me alive if you want."

"I won't let you out of those chains, just so you know. So if you want to fuck your personal little hooker Janine, it will have to be here, in this dungeon, with you in those chains."

"Call her a hooker again, and I'll rip your tongue out of your filthy mouth, if it's the last thing I do."

Lorenzo folds his arms across his chest, planting his feet apart. He's tall and lean, leaner than the two wolves with sleek black fur flanking him, but I know he's stronger than both.

"You know what I did after you hi-jacked my imprinting ceremony with Janine by stealing her away? I ordered my men to kill her on sight."

I jerk against the chains, spitting menacingly through my teeth. "If you as much as think that again—"

"Oh no, I only thought it once. I have new plans now, let me tell you about them." He leans forward from his waist. "And let me start with the beginning. When you stole Janine away, I was devastated. I cried like a groom left at the altar—in the end, that's sort of what I was."

"No, it isn't, because you hadn't lost a woman you loved. You'd lost a woman you needed."

"Does that really make a difference? I hung on her, just as you did. I needed her to create an army of werewolves, while you needed her because you were desperate to dip your cock inside of her. But it was need for both of us."

My knuckles show white as I ball my fists. "I could punch your pretty face till there was nothing left of it. But you're not stupid enough to face me in a fair fight, are you?"

"You thought I wouldn't be clever enough to find you," he says. "But guess what—I was clever enough to seek out the whore you hooked up with. I caught your scent inside that filthy establishment, but then surprise—further trails joined it. The scent of Janine Kovesi, and the smell of the two of you *fucking*." He roars the last word, his cheeks alight with fury.

"As I stared at that ravished bed stained with both of your pleasure I wanted to kill her," he spits. "Even more than I wanted to kill you. But I wouldn't lay a hand on her, not while you still have what I want most in the world."

"The Reaper's weapon. You'll bargain for that?"

"There will be no bargain. You will cede it to me, or Janine dies."

"And what guarantee do I have that you'll keep her alive after I turn over the weapon."

"You're in my power, Conan, and so is the woman you love. You don't get to set terms."

"I want to have her again," I say, loud and clear so that the werewolves in the shadows hear it, too. I catch Cinzia's scent, so I guess she's here somewhere in here as well. "I want to make love to her."

"And then you'll give it over to me without further ado?"

"Then I want a guarantee that you'll send her safely to my brother Nero. Then I will give it over."

A vicious thought crosses his pale blue eyes. "No further requests? This is all you want?"

"All I want."

"What about all the damage you cost me by imprinting on the woman I needed to create my army? Who's gonna pay for that loss, and how?"

"I tried to resist the need to be with her, but I just couldn't. She threatened that she would find another werewolf and let him, a stranger, imprint on her before either of us could, and I just... I lost it. I couldn't imagine her with another man, I wanted to smash faces and break necks. Believe it or not, it wasn't personal." My arms strain so hard the chains rattle, and Lorenzo's wolves stand to attention.

"Bring the girl," Lorenzo commands.

Janine

TEARS STREAM DOWN MY face as I'm forced to look at the man I love hanging from heavy chains, blood and bruises crisscrossing his muscular body.

"Ever thought you'd see the powerful Conan Wolf in such a situation, Janine?" Lorenzo whispers in my ear, brushing my hair away. My skin crawls at the touch of his breath on my skin. "These chains, they're made of special iron, imbued with sacred chemistry by the Witch Eyed Sisters. When Cinzia, their leader, betrayed the Wolf pack, the entire Order did. The chains keep the wolf in check, so he won't be able to shift and defend himself no matter what we do to him."

I glance over at Cinzia, who's staring at me from under her red hood. "The things that a scorned woman would do, isn't it?" I manage, but look away from her immediately, as if she's not worthy of another glance.

I focus on Conan's reddish eyes. Strange. He's much too still, too quiet for a man in trouble, almost as if he has a plan to save us both. My brain must be playing tricks on me, clawing to a hope of salvation that I know we don't have.

"At least I know you'll never get your army," I defy Lorenzo, feeling his presence behind me. "I'm Conan's bonded mate. If I ever make werewolves, they will answer to him, and not you."

"Never say never, Janine. It hurt to lose you, it's true, but maybe I'll meet someone like you again someday. But you know what, it doesn't matter, because that's not why I brought you here."

He winds an arm around my shoulders. I try to shake it off, but he pushes me closer to Conan until the rusty scent of his blood crawls up my nostrils. I can't keep back the tears as I look up into his face. His hard features, his dangerous stare, and the scar that runs down his cheek used to turn me on, but now that I love the man behind all that, my heart breaks. There was so much pain in his life, and now this.

"Conan and I have reached an arrangement, Janine," Lorenzo says. "He agreed to cede The Reaper's weapon to me, if I granted him two wishes—he wants to make love to you one last time before he dies, and see you safely back under his brother Nero's protection."

"Die," I repeat, hot tears rolling down my cheeks. I press my lips together, tasting the salt as they touch my mouth.

"It's the reason I had you take a bath of milk and roses just before. So he can enjoy your skin at its softest."

"So kind of you," I hiss.

"Contrary to what you might think, I'm not a monster."

"No. You're a worthless piece of shit."

I can feel his anger stabbing my back, but I don't move an inch, keeping my eyes on Conan and making myself a promise. If Lorenzo kills Conan, I'll be left with only one reason to go on living—I'll build the army of werewolves that Lorenzo so ardently desires, I'll sleep with a thousand men if I have to, but I'll build it for Nero. So that he can take down the Piovra pack once and for all.

"Now," Lorenzo says, running his hand over the side of the red lace negligee he's had me wear. "You'll go to your lover, drop to your knees and suck his cock. Right here, in front of us all."

"Say what?!"

"Son of a bitch," Conan roars, the chains rattling as he pulls at them. Dust and stones break away from the walls, and the werewolves stand to attention, ready to step in if he manages to break free.

"I don't have to watch this," Cinzia says and makes to leave, but Lorenzo stops her with a hand on her elbow.

"Oh, you will watch, witch sister. Didn't you say you wanted to see the human humiliated?"

"Yes, but he loves her," she spits through her teeth, jerking her head in Conan's direction. "I don't want to witness their love again. Because it will be love making, even under these circumstances."

"You. Will. Watch," Lorenzo decrees.

All the werewolves' eyes switch to me from the darkness as I stand in front of Conan in the cone of moonlight from the opening above our heads. I look up into the moonlight, and realize that it's a full moon, the third one, and maybe I can help him set his wolf free. If what he told me is true, then his wolf has full power on the night of the third full moon, and he might be able to save himself if I manage to help him.

"I'll do it." My whisper bounces off the walls in the hungry silence. "But first, let me make you a promise, Lorenzo. I will see your pack wiped out from the face of the earth if it's the last thing I do."

"And how do you plan to do that?" he mocks as a ripple of laughter travels among the gathered werewolves in the darkness.

"The same way you would—by going as low as I have to."

"I'm proud of you, Janine. You just made the first good decision since you and I met."

"I suppose that's what revenge requires."

"It's what intelligence requires. And, if anything, you're one brilliant woman. I love myself a brilliant woman. Maybe, one day, after you've grieved enough from the death of your lover, you'll consider going out with me?"

"Be careful what you wish for." I glare at him with the promise of death.

He snaps his fingers, and two wolves bring chairs from the back. He takes a seat on one, pulling Cinzia's hand and forcing her to take a seat on the other.

"Begin," he commands. "On your knees, and take him in your mouth."

I turn my back to him, slowly, hearing my own breath inside my head. I try to focus on Conan, and forget about the spectators behind me. His loving gaze set on my face helps. He whispers, very low,

"Trust me." He leans his beautiful face closer. "I love you."

He leans to me as low as he can as I stand on my tiptoes, craning my neck to press my hot lips to his. God, they feel hard and cold like rock. I cup his strong jaw with my trembling hands, caressing my way to the back of his neck, needing him like air, my tongue sliding between his lips.

He opens his mouth, his tongue meeting mine. My blood starts to boil, and I forget my surroundings, caressing him all over. My hands glide down his shoulders to his pectorals, my fingers splayed to feel all of him, but then I feel crusty crevices under my palms. I break the deep kiss, looking down at cuts with dry blood.

"Don't stop," he whispers with his eyes half-closed. "Your touch is healing me."

The blood no longer pours out of his wounds, the cuts healing right before my eyes.

"On your knees," Lorenzo commands angrily from behind. He's losing his patience—in the end, I imagine he didn't come here to watch tender love-making, but dirty fuckery. I glance back to see him bent forward, pale blue eyes glinting like glass.

I bend down slowly until I feel the cold stone under my knees, the chains rattling as Conan moves. His naked cock is already engorged and ready for me. I wrap my hand gently around it, making Conan pull at the chains, hissing with emotion. I move my head to the side just enough for Lorenzo to see the mighty member between Conan's legs.

"I love how big you are," I tell Conan, loud enough for Lorenzo and Cinzia to hear. "When you fucked me, I could feel you so deep."

With my head still to the side I lick slowly around the engorged purple head, causing Conan to push his hips forward, taking in the pleasure and searching for the heat of my mouth. Hisses of excitement run through the gathered werewolves. One of them howls, but I know Lorenzo wouldn't let any of them take me, because he fears a change of allegiance. I know I'm safe from rape, all they can do is watch and suffer because they can never have me.

I open my mouth and take the head of Conan's dick inside, then lick it like it's a lollipop, keeping my head in a position that allows the spectators to see everything.

Lorenzo intended to humiliate me by having me fucked in front of all his people, but his plan backfired deliciously, and I will make it even more so. Keeping one hand firmly on the root of Conan's cock I move my mouth to his balls, sticking my tongue out to lick them.

I take my free hand to my butt, and hook one finger into the red lace thong, moving it aside and pushing my butt back to expose both my crack and my asshole. Wolves howl, starting to lose control, and forcing Lorenzo to call, "Quiet!" They obey, but I won't make this easy on Lorenzo. I wrap my lips around Conan's huge cock, slowly working my jaw wider and sliding down to the root. At the same time I sink my finger inside my pussy, exposed in such a way that they can all see.

The wolves make noise, forcing Lorenzo to demand silence again, but then I take it up a notch and stick my thumb inside my ass. The wolves lose it, forcing Lorenzo to stand and shout orders at them. I can't see what's happening behind me, but I hear the commotion, the punches, the thuds, the cracking. Lorenzo and his most trusted wolves must be fighting to keep the others away from me, which gives me the chance to try and free Conan. But when I try to get up he says,

"Don't stop." He looks down at me with eyes that could eat me alive, a god with encrusted blood all over him, in chains, waiting to be pleasured by me as if it can free him. "Trust me, I know what I'm doing, and it will save both of us. Just don't stop."

I glance behind only when I hear Cinzia moan, and discover her being fucked by two wolves in their shifted forms, and enjoying it. One is taking her mouth, claws in her dark hair, while the other slams into her pussy from behind like there's no tomorrow. A third one comes into the picture, ripping her red hood to pieces, and grabbing her breasts. She's enjoying it like a nympho right now, but I have a feeling she'll be hating herself tomorrow, which is the best revenge I can think of.

I look up at the man I'm serving on my knees, a god in chains. I rise up to my feet and practically climb up him, lowering my pussy down on his cock. I'm so wet that I can take him all in, my walls slick but tight around him. I hold on to his shoulders, sliding slowly up and down his length, our eyes locked with each other.

We must be quite a sight from behind, a little blonde with only a red lace bra around her tits riding a beast chained by his wrists and his ankles. A dirty show they can watch, but never touch, because it could mean that the little blonde fucking the beast becomes their new master. I hear Lorenzo screaming at them like a primadonna with hysteria, and I feel an urge to see him, to enjoy his despair, while taking my orgasm from my lover.

"Will you take me from behind," I whisper to Conan, my face hot.

"Yes," he whispers, completely taken with me. I kiss him deeply and climb down his firm body. I turn around, facing a mess of wolves and men.

The first thing that jumps out at me is Cinzia, completely naked and sweaty being roughly used by a man in leather who rubs his balls on her mouth.

Conan bends his knees to bring himself to the level of my naked buttocks. I bend forward and reach between my legs, guiding his mighty cock to my pussy. I'm sore from riding him, but also wet to my thighs, and needing to climax.

I push back on him until his cock fills me, screaming with pain and pleasure. The wolves have stopped doing what they were doing and are now watching. I open my bra, letting my breasts bounce freely as I pump myself hard against Conan. Lorenzo watches with an open mouth and, the moment my eyes rest on his, I feel it.

Conan's throbbing cock parts my walls, causing me an explosive orgasm. He spills his seed inside of me, but it's more than that—it's power, pure white, bright light shooting through every little vein in my body. I feel it prickling underneath the skin of my scalp, stretching the skin on my fingers, my bones, my fingernails.

"I. Will. You. My. Power." With those words Conan pours all of his essence inside of me, growling his orgasm like a beast in a rage.

"No," Lorenzo cries, stretching out his hand as if he wants to grab me. That's the last thing I see before the bright white light penetrates every cell of my body, shutting down my brain.

Janine

WHEN I COME BACK TO myself, the place is bathed in complete silence. And darkness, at first. The room has tilted with me, and now I'm lying naked on my side on the cold stone floor, Conan's seed trickling from between my folds onto my thigh. The moon has disappeared, as if the night swallowed it whole.

I push myself up onto my hands, trying to kick-start my brain, but the first organs that react are my ears. They adjust like the ears of a wolf, picking up on the breathing around. Then I catch scents, singling out wet dog fur, sweat, arousal, and a whole lot of fucking. And Lorenzo.

My nose curls as I sniff for his location. I get up to my feet—it's much easier and smoother than I expected it to be after the wild way I fucked my lover. My sight clears as I follow the trail of Lorenzo's scent, finding him on his knees, head down. I stare down at him in his black robe that makes him look so much like a raven.

"You should probably check on your lover," he grunts without looking up at me. I can smell his body chemistry, and I translate it on some strange level—this isn't a resigned man, it's an angry one.

"Conan is fine." I can feel him as if he's part of my body. I know he's behind me, and that he's broken his chains. The power of his orgasm fueled him, and he shattered them with a roar just before I collapsed, and the hall went dark. Now he stands still behind me in the same spot, breathing steadily.

"You, on the other hand." I start pacing around Lorenzo, my moves as sleek as a panther's. Everything I do comes from some new and strange instinct. "You seem troubled."

He laughs like a mad man, coming up on his knees and leaning his head back. I can see his face as if there were light in the hall, even though it's pitch black. Another very strange new ability?

"The Reaper's weapon," Lorenzo grunts through his teeth. "It can only be earned or given. And he gave it to *you*. That's what he'd planned all along, the fffffffucker. In the Witch Eyed Sisters' chains he couldn't shift or use the power, but he could transfer it to you. Then he used the momentum to break the chains. All of a sudden, there were two wielders of the secret weapon in the room."

Before I can wrap my mind around this Conan takes over.

"You thought yourself the big strategist," he says in his deep, sexy voice that fills the stone hall. "When in truth you were being a fool."

"You played me like a fucking idiot," Lorenzo growls. "You asked to make love to her one last time so that you could give her your power. And since she is your bonded mate, she shares it with you." His whole body shakes with the nervous laugh of a madman. "Now she can suck the strength from every werewolf in this room. We could kill her, if she were alone, but with you to back her up...."

I look down at myself as I become aware of what happened. Jesus! I have long, wolfish fingers and claws, my skin like taut, smooth leather. Fuck, I'm a beast! I turn around swiftly and see myself reflected in Conan's eyes—a nymph made of black leather, only her hair shining white. The long dark claws seem made of sharp bone.

"Jesus Christ," I whisper.

Conan caresses my face, staring at me full of love. There are tears in his eyes.

"You're so beautiful, Janine Kovesi," he drawls. "Queen of the Werewolves."

A rustle goes through the entire hall, and werewolves fall to their knees.

"The Reaper's secret weapon," Conan explains, taking my hand and lacing his fingers with mine, "is the ability to suck the power out of werewolves. He left it in a chalice in his abandoned hideout two hundred years ago, and I think he did it on purpose—to sow discord between the two leaders hunting him down, Lorenzo and me."

"But," I mutter. "That means that he, The Reaper, also has this power."

"No, because The Reaper is a serpent. Only werewolves can make use of this ability." He smiles at me. "Or a werewolf's bonded mate."

I look at myself again, staggered. I barely even dare to ask, "Am I now a werewolf now?" My voice is a mere whisper.

"Not exactly, but.... The Old Lore that I studied after I got the power said that in the very unlikely case a Fated Female received this ability, she would become a shape-shifter, but that she would shift only on full-moon nights." He looks at Lorenzo. "That's why I asked to have Janine again tonight."

A nasty growl breaks out of Lorenzo's chest. Something has changed about him, but I can't put my finger on what until he bares his teeth that morph into fangs. His eyes start glowing, and dark thorns push out of his skin until I realize it's thick, bristly black fur. He grows bigger while he's in the air, throwing himself at me.

In a split second the wolf form of Conan springs to life, as if rolling out of his skin, scattering it in the process. The two big wolves meet midair, slamming into each other, then falling to the ground like a huge clump of fur.

"Conan," I cry as they break apart but tense to attack again, fangs bared and claws curved. They're ready to slice each other's throats.

"She may have the ability to drain the wolves of their power," Lorenzo hisses, his words barely understandable if it weren't for my new shape-shifter senses. "But I will take you down with me, Conan Wolf, if it's the last thing I do." He addresses his men. "Take her down!"

But none of them reacts.

"They just witnessed the birth of a queen," Cinzia says. "They won't attack her, at least not until you win this fight, Lorenzo."

She hovers in a corner with some guy's jacket around her. Her hair is messy, but her cheeks are bright, and you know what? She seems satisfied, and even smiles when she looks at me.

A thud against the wall makes my head snap in its direction, the ground shaking under us. Lorenzo has thrown Conan against the wall. I move toward them, but Conan shoots back to his feet so fast a gust of air hits my face.

"No, my queen." He advances on Lorenzo. "This one's mine."

They move around each other in a circle, focused, not even blinking as they take one smooth step at a time.

"I could have gotten over anything you might have done to me," Conan says. "But you wanted to humiliate Janine and break her spirit by using her in the dirtiest ways. For that I'll make your death particularly careful."

I can sense their power radiating off their devil-like bodies, Conan a huge muscular brown beast, and Lorenzo a long, lean animal with black spiked fur. He loses the stare-down and his patience, launching himself at Conan, who sidesteps his punch, sending an upper cut right under his chin.

Lorenzo's jaw cracks, and he growls in excruciating pain. He stumbles forward, Conan moving out of his way. He flashes behind Lorenzo, grabs his furry neck and drives him full-force into the wall. I wince at the bang, chunks of bare stone smashing against the ground, Lorenzo's limp body falling over them. There's a hole in the wall where his head drilled through. Fuck, Conan is one hell of a beast.

He lifts Lorenzo off the ground, displaying him like a hanging rag to his own men.

"This is what is left of your leader." He morphs back into a human as he speaks out loud. "A semi-unconscious stray dog with blood dripping out of his split mouth. If you choose to follow him regardless, you're free to join him in the dungeons under the Doge's palace, because we're retaking them, and that's where he's going. But if you wish to replace your loyalties, this is the time to do it."

Wolves exchange glances with each other, but decide to step forward and kneel down one by one. Just as the last and most hesitant-looking shifter steps forward to bend the knee, Lorenzo snaps out of his lethargy and slashes his claws at Conan's throat with a war cry.

Time stands still, and the blood freezes in my veins. My mouth opens slowly as the moment stretches into an eternity, and I'm certain this is it. No one will have the time to intervene before those rough black claws slide across my lover's throat. I watch those claws as they pierce skin and muscle, blood swelling out, coating them.

But something doesn't fit. It's not the amount of bleeding you would expect from a sliced throat. I focus on the wound—it's not Conan's throat, but his forearm. He's blocked Lorenzo's attack, and now he glares at him with bloodlust in his red eyes.

I can see the decision in his stare before he makes it. He throws Lorenzo to the wall, pins him there with a knee on his stomach, then grabs his head in both of his huge hands, and pulls.

My head snaps away from the carnage as blood squirts out of the black wolf's throat, where his head used to be—Conan ripped it off his shoulders. Gasps and hisses ring out among the gathered wolves, some of them shifting and howling. Slowly, the moon creeps back in through the opening above the place where Conan had been hanging in chains. The eclipse is over.

CHAPTER VII

Janine

I can't say I'm surprised when Cinzia knocks on my door.

"I've been expecting you." I've just emerged out of a hot bath, and I'm towel-drying my hair as I invite her to move away from the door and come closer.

"I, I wanted to apologize." She wrings her hands in front of her lap.

"For what?" I throw the towel on the bed, and strip off the bathrobe in front of her, reaching for the satin nightgown. "Betraying both Conan and me, or for wanting to watch me being humiliated. I could still have your head, you know."

"You have every reason to hate me, and I understand that you do."

I walk to the table on the balcony—we're at Lorenzo's palazzo, now that his werewolves are basically my subjects—and pour myself some tea. The breeze is pleasant, the cozily lit gondolas and the lovers' bridge make for an exquisite atmosphere, but I can't enjoy them as I normally would. I still have to recover from the shock.

"But please understand," Cinzia says, following me to the balcony, "Lorenzo Piovra didn't leave me a choice."

"I'm sorry, but I don't buy that." I lean against the wrought iron banister with a cup of tea in my hand. "You told Conan something completely different. That you did it out of spite, for revenge because he preferred me to you."

"But Lorenzo had also discovered the establishment. He would have killed me and all of my Witch Eyed Sisters if I didn't help him. Now circumstances have changed, and if you choose to kill me, that's fine. But please spare the rest of the Order."

"You surely understand that we can never trust the Witch Eyed Sisters again."

She doesn't reply, just keeps her head down. I narrow my eyes, trying to read her motives.

"You and your sisters, you don't really know loyalty, do you? You're just going along with the most powerful."

"With all due respect, the most powerful could easily destroy us. What would you have had the Order do when Lorenzo came? What do you think would have happened if we refused to help?"

She has a point, I must admit. I stand here looking at her, trying to put myself in her shoes. The only man who ever showed her some measure of respect was Conan—or so I gathered from what I've been told. She knew this man could never love her, but she thought she could love enough for both of them. When he imprinted on me, even though he'd always professed he'd never imprint on anyone, she felt betrayed. Then Lorenzo came and put her and her Order sisters under pressure. Maybe this really wasn't entirely about personal vendetta or hatred.

"Cinzia, I'm sure that, had you been a Fated Female, Conan would have fallen for you instead of me. I really wish that you get the love that you desire as much as you desired Conan."

"Actually," she whispers as if she barely has the guts to admit it, "I don't think I'm made for being with just one man."

"Oh..." I think I understand where she's going. "How many men took you back in the dungeons?"

Her face heats up to the tips of her ears.

"How many?" I encourage her when she hesitates.

"Four. But I enjoyed it more than I expected." Her whole face goes an even deeper shade of red.

"Would you like to see them again? Maybe a harem becomes you."

"What do you mean?" Her eyes snap up at me, full of surprise.

"I mean..." I look out at the canal, not sure how to go about this. "Would you like to, like, get to know them better?"

"I'm not sure. I don't think they have a very good opinion of me."

"Why do you think that?"

She snorts. "Are you kidding? I'm a hooker by profession, and I did it with the four of them at the same time."

"When we returned to the palazzo, I noticed four men very close to you. It seemed to me they were protecting you. If those were the men who took you, I think they're fonder of you than you might expect. I think a bond was formed there."

She raises her eyebrows. "If it did, then it's a very strange bond."

"I will arrange for you to meet again."

She shakes her head and smiles awkwardly. "I can't imagine looking into their faces. The things they must think of me..."

"I told you, I saw them around you. They all stared at you the way infatuated boys stare at the most popular girl in school."

"Yes, but unlike the popular girl, I'm not someone you can take out to family dinners and introduce to your friends. All their friends here know who I am, and what I do for a living."

"Used to. What you *used to* do for a living, because you won't be doing it from now on."

"Excuse me?"

I smile. "I want you in my service. You'll be my own personal witch."

"Actually, I don't see how—"

"Think about it." I pour her some tea and hand her the cup. "Now that the Wolves and the Piovras have united, we stand a good chance to defeat the serpents. Sadly, the Reaper's weapon that both Conan and I now wield doesn't help us in this war, because it's only designed for us to annihilate wolves. But you are a witch. I saw you erase a man's memory and put him to sleep only with only words, and covering Conan and my scent with a perfume you designed. Cinzia, I think your talents are too valuable to waste away in a brothel."

"Wow." She stares at me, leaning against the wrought iron banister across from me on the little balcony. "I think that's the nicest thing anyone has ever said to me."

"And you'll hear much more if you accept my invitation. I'd like to have you close, which means I'd like you to come along to Darkwood Falls. But only if you want you. I'd never dream of making you."

She smiles. "Conan was right to fall in love with you. You are queen material."

"Thank you. Will you take my offer?"

"I wish you'd discussed that offer with me first," Conan's deep voice fills the air. How didn't I hear him come in? He heads over from the room, joining us on the balcony.

Cinzia bends her head as if she's seen the king.

"Leave us," Conan commands. "We'll talk about this in the morning, all of us. Now Janine needs rest before she makes other hasty decisions."

Cinzia leaves, while I stay behind on the balcony, pouring myself another cup of tea. Conan made her insecure about the position I offered, and I don't like it. She'd gotten her hopes high, and I want them to stay that way.

"I don't appreciate you intervening when I'm discussing things with people," I say, trying to avoid his gaze. "Or when I promise them something."

He changes the subject, his gaze burning the side of my face. "You've been avoiding me since the dungeon. Why?"

"You have to ask?" I place the cup of tea on the saucer and turn with my back to him, looking out at the lovers' bridge. I grip the banister with both hands, trying to control my emotions before they spin out of control. "I watched you rip a werewolf's head off, Conan. I can't get that image out of my head, it's what I see every time I look at you."

"But you are my bonded mate. Sooner or later you will have to look at me again." He traps me between his powerful arms that he places them on the banister on each side of mine, his muscular chest touching my shoulder blades. I close my eyes tightly, struggling to ignore the butterflies it stirs in my stomach.

"Why offer Cinzia a place so close to us? She betrayed us once, and she almost admitted she might do it again."

"You were listening?"

"I was in the room next to yours."

"The possibility of her betraying us again is one of the reasons I want to have her close. There's more, actually. I would have her reinstated as head of the Witch Eyed Sisters, and named High Priestess."

Conan laughs, the sound of it deep and dark, his chest vibrating against my back. "High Priestess is a rather paradoxical title, wouldn't you say, considering what she does—or used to do?"

"First of all, I don't like your tone regarding the woman's choices. Those are hers alone and don't make her any less of a great woman. Cinzia has power, and I think we can use that to our advantage. Besides, I want her to lead the Order because that way they won't make a move without us knowing. In Darkwood Falls she'll lead the kind of life she secretly craves, and that will strengthen her loyalty to us."

"Hmmm, I hear sass behind those words." He pushes his body into mine, bending his knees enough for me to feel his rock-hard cock against my buttocks. I grip tighter to the banister, but manage to resist my arousal. His scent and the warmth of his body are enough to get me wet, and it drives me crazy because he's irresistible.

"I think four of the Piovra werewolves are infatuated with her. If we take them along, she will be thoroughly entertained, and constantly satisfied. Still, I don't appreciate eavesdropping either. If you wanted to take part in our conversation, you should have stepped in from the beginning."

"I wasn't interested in your conversation," he says in my ear, his lips brushing my earlobe. "Actually, I wasn't even actively listening. I was too busy doing something else."

"Namely what?"

"Imagining what it would feel like to make you mine on this balcony overlooking Venice." He grinds himself slowly against my buttocks as he talks, his voice a deep drawl.

I can't fight this, I'm helpless against his touch. I push myself against his rock hard dick, letting it rub between my buttocks though the satin. My eyes roll back as I take in the sensation.

I don't know at what point he freed his erection, but when I feel him naked and hot through the satin, my heart jumps—he's really going to fuck me, right here, on this balcony.

His rough hand grazes its way up my leg, and sinks in my panties. We both hiss as he pushes two fingers between my soaked folds, sliding through my cream over my clit, while he lifts my gown off my butt with the other hand.

"Conan, people are watching," I manage hoarsely, looking at the couples on the lovers' bridge.

"Seems it's become a motif in our love story," he says in my ear, sliding his cock from behind through my cream, then guiding it between my buttocks. "And to be honest, I find it to my liking."

I moan in delight, even though I've never done this before.

"Soon," he says, his voice gruff with anticipation, "I will do you on that bridge, and I won't care how many people stroll on it and stare."

"Can't they punish us by law for having sex in public?"

"Only if they catch us."

He pushes the large head of his cock into my hole, and I wince. "You're big, Conan." But that's all the protest I manage. We are bonded mates now, I love him to the point of insanity, and I think he feels the same. That means that I want him in all ways and at all times, even if it's anal sex, and the first time I ever try it.

"I'll be gentle," he whispers. He's already panting, his muscles tight with restrained desire, but he keeps making me wet with his hand inside my pussy, and dipping his cock in my cream to make it more comfortable between my buttocks.

Soon he's sliding easily inside my ass, while his fingers pump my pussy. I white-knuckle the banister, my breasts swaying until they emerge from the satin. Soon, people are taking snapshots of a couple fucking like animals on a Venetian balcony. A woman in what looks like a satin toga that doesn't do anything to hide her swaying breasts, being fucked in the ass by a big guy, while he's also pumping her pussy with his hand. She's got a foot up on a wrought iron chair to enable easier access for him.

I'm not surprised to find those pictures on the internet the next day, nor bothered—Conan has kept a grip on my jaw and my head tilted backwards, to him, so that no one could take a picture of my face, while also hiding his in my hair. By the time we land on obscure porn sites we're already on a plane over the ocean, heading back to Darkwood Falls. And looking forward to watching the videos.

Conan

NERO PULLS ME IN A bear hug while the others slap my back.

"So good to have you home, Big Brozzer," Achilles says with his rowdy grin. Right next to the boys, Arianna and Princess are opening their arms to receive Janine.

"Who would have thought a little over a year ago," Nero says as he invites me inside Princess's huge manor, where they're preparing their wedding. "That three women from Darkwood Falls who grew up as sisters would marry three werewolf brothers."

"You asked her, right?" Achilles chimes in. "To marry you?"

"Yes, of course I have." On a balcony in Venice, right after we put on a porn show for the tourists, but I keep that part to myself.

"Maybe we can have a double wedding," Nero says. "I'm sure Princess wouldn't mind."

"Plus that it would really fit," Drago puts in. "Nero the alpha marrying his secretary, double wedding alongside Janine Kovesi, marrying her bodyguard."

All laugh, but when we reach the cozy sitting room full of old books, secret doors behind wooden bookcases, and good old scotch, Hercules makes his entrance, hungry for answers.

"Lady of the Reaper's secret weapon," he says, dropping his tattooed bulk that's even larger than mine into the nearest armchair. "Doesn't that basically mean that she can wipe out all of us? She can suck the power out of werewolves, am I right?"

"Nothing to be afraid of, Hercules," I explain. "She can drain any werewolf that's not of the Wolf pack—because she's mated to one of us. But there's more—she can also *make* werewolves."

"I was a bit taken aback when I first heard that," Nero says. "And a bit frustrated. I wished I would have thought of investigating the girls' one night stands after we became protectors of Darkwood Falls."

"Don't sweat it, Nero," I appease him. "You have to be a deranged bastard like Lorenzo to think of stuff like that."

Nero smiles. "You've changed, brother."

I smile back. "I'm in love."

"But one thing I don't understand," Hercules pokes. "If you transferred your power to Janine, and she's now Queen of the Werewolves, then why weren't you King of the Werewolves when you wielded it?"

"It's the special superpower that she had even before all of this happened," Nero explains in my place.

"She could practically make werewolves by—" I bite my lip because I really hate saying this, which I can tell two of my brothers can understand. "Exchanging body fluids with them. Can I have a drink, Nero?"

"Sure." He hurries over to make me one, because he knows what it's like to think about your bonded mate doing it with other men. The rage and hurt that shoots through me, I could demolish the whole house.

"That means that she can now *unmake* wolves, wielding the Reaper's weapon," I explain after I down my drink. "And easily, because her chemistry transformed the gift when I transferred it over."

"And that's not even the most interesting part," Nero tells our brothers as he takes a seat on the couch. "But the fact that Conan still retains his power. He can drain werewolves of their strength."

"Smart of you, Big Brozzer." Achilles slaps my back. "To give over your power to your bonded mate. It's also a burden that you can now share."

"It wasn't my intention. I would have given Janine everything—my power, my life, my soul, but not this burden."

"I'll be honest." Achilles relaxes back in his chair, resting an ankle on his knee. He's an audacious young fuck. "I wouldn't want to be in any of your guys' place. Falling in love like that, to the point of losing your minds, it's like putting yourself in prison."

"It's what I used to think," I admit. "But it's the greatest thing that's ever happened to me."

"Yes, what can I say, but that I wish you a happy eternity of bondage," Achilles mocks, running a hand though his hair. "And I say this with all due respect for your mates, who have sort of become my sisters."

Janine walks into the room. "Sorry for crashing your boy talk, but dinner is ready. Princess's mom is joining, and she doesn't tolerate delays."

Nero jumps off of his chair. "What, Princess's mother is here?"

"You've never met her?" Janine inquires as she takes her rightful place on my lap.

"No, actually, just her dad, who still spends all his time in his chambers. I would have taken Princess away to avoid the situation, but she insisted that we stayed and watched over him."

"I think that's why her mom came back today—the way I know Melanthe, she wanted not only to meet you, but also to make her husband accept you."

"He doesn't really have a choice," Nero blocks.

"Melanthe," Achilles says. "An interesting name. Almost as eccentric as Princess."

"And twice as eccentric a woman," Janine assures him. "She locked herself in her room after she arrived, surely because she wants to make a grand entrance this evening. Let us head to the dining room already. The girls are already there."

Nero and Drago lead the way, eager to be close to their mates again. I lag behind, hand in hand with my Janine.

Princess's mother takes her sweet time, being late to her own party like the diva we all expect her to be, so Janine and I tell the story of what happened in detail, leaving only the graphic description of our love-making out.

"You killed Lorenzo Piovra and gained control over his entire pack," Achilles sums it up appreciatively. "But the Piovra pack are like a nuke. You need someone you can trust on site, make sure they don't do anything stupid."

"I left my some of my best men there," I tell him. "But they expect backup in a couple of days."

"I'll see to it," Nero says.

A scream tears through the house like the chill of a ghost. With only a glance at each other, my brothers and I throw back our chairs and run up the main stairs, following it. Nero tears down the door to Charles Skye's dark chamber, searching for the trouble using his werewolf vision. Janine gasps by my side, because she can see it as well with her new senses. But Princess and Arianna can't.

So Princess hits the lights, inhales sharply, and sways on her feet. Luckily Nero is right behind her when her eyes roll back, and she loses consciousness, falling limp into his arms.

Charles Skye sits in his wheelchair, his head tilted grotesquely back, his throat a gaping wound. I can understand it's a shocking sight to both Princess and her mother, Melanthe—because I suppose that's who the woman in the eccentric golden dress is—but it's what Janine does that shocks me.

She starts to breathe heavily. I put my hands around her to steady her, talking to her to calm her down, but her skin begins morphing into that of the Queen—the sleek, smooth leather-like skin, her fingernails transforming into black bone claws. In only a few moments the Queen springs out the open window, chasing something in the night.

I shift, my wolf shattering my skin and my clothes, and jumping after her. The entire pack follows, save for Nero.

When we return, half an hour later, we find Nero and the two women in the drawing room, where Melanthe stares at her hands in shock, as if she had blood on them, though they're perfectly clean. Her elegant face is blank, expressing nothing.

"Did you find him?" Princess cries with pain in her voice. Her face is hot, her eyes puffy, her red locks messy from all the times she's pulled at them. Nero stands behind her, hands on her shoulders. If he weren't here, exerting the power of his love on her, I'm sure she'd collapse and drown in her pain.

"We caught the trail of a serpent, but also mixed with human," I explain as Janine laces her fingers with mine. She's retaken her human form easily, somewhere in the middle of the forest. "I had to abandon the chase because of Janine. She shape-shifted automatically when she sensed the trail of the killer, but when she lost it she couldn't keep her Queen form. I had to return and protect her."

"I might have something," Achilles's voice reaches us from the front door, which he's just thrown open. He comes into the room, still in the process of shifting back from a wolf with metallic bluish-black fur into the tattooed male model.

What he holds up raises more questions than it brings answers. It's shed reptilian skin, but it's special. It's heavily scaled, which means whatever attacked Charles Skye was either an old serpent, or maybe another kind of shifter. Something far deadlier than an average serpent. One thing is certain, though—whatever shifter it was, this was a person from town. A shifter we don't know about.

At least we know where to start—determining who had a motive to kill Charles Skye. Except many people had a reason to kill him. The serpents, because he'd betrayed them. In the end, he was the alpha's father-in-law. An alpha he didn't actually fully accept, so Nero could theoretically have had him killed as well, but all of us know he would have never done that to Princess. And when my brothers and I gather in the dinning room to talk about this in detail without the women, Achilles snaps.

"Am I missing something here? Why are we leaving out our main suspect?" he says, and we all follow his gaze to Melanthe, who is still in our field of vision through the open doors to the drawing room. The woman is still staring at her hands, saying nothing. I doubt she's even aware of us.

"We all waited for her to come down the entire evening, haven't we? We were all downstairs dining when this happened—except for her."

"She was here the whole time, Achilles, she's not the one who shed the skin you found," I argue.

"No, but she might not be working alone. Maybe the killer acted on her orders."

"The main suspect indeed." Janine walks in. She must have heard us with her now sharpened senses. "It was so obviously her, that it can't be true. If you ask me, only one thing is obvious—whoever did it, they wanted it to look like it was Melanthe." She looks up at me. "I think I have an idea how to solve this mystery, but we can't do it without this woman, and we need someone to monitor her at all times."

"Are you saying she needs a bodyguard?" I say.

"Yes, but not quite the kind of bodyguard you were for me. It must be a secret bodyguard. A ghost, a shadow." She looks at the mentally absent woman. "Not even she needs to know about him. Whoever is trying to set her up is gonna try again when they see it didn't work the first time, and when they do, we have to be prepared."

"I like that idea," Nero says. He looks around. "Any volunteers?"

THE END

Enjoyed this story? Let the world know. Leave a review, and tell people what you think.

https://www.amazon.com/dp/B07VJBXVZH

Also, if you want to receive a notification as soon as a new book hits the Zon, sign up to Ana Calin's Newsletter here, and you'll be the first to know.

If you loved this book and can't wait for the next one, guess what? You don't have to wait. *In Sin with the Wolf* is already available for you here:

Find the first two books of the series here:

If you need more paranormal love to fill your time until the next release, enjoy the Dracula's Bloodline series (five books already out!), available on Amazon now:

Printed in Great Britain
by Amazon